Yiza

Published in 2017 by
Haus Publishing Ltd
70 Cadogan Place
London SW1X 9AH
www.hauspublishing.com

First published in 2016 by Carl Hanser Verlag as *Das Mädchen mit dem Fingerhut*

A CIP catalogue record for this book is available from the British Library

ISBN: 978-1-910376-75-1
eISBN: 978-1-910376-76-8

Typeset in Garamond by MacGuru Ltd

Yiza

Michael Köhlmeier

Translated by Ruth Martin

MICHAEL KÖHLMEIER is an Austrian writer and musician. He divides his time between Hohenems in Vorarlberg and Vienna. The recipient of many prizes and awards in his native Austria, his novel *Two Gentlemen on the Beach* (2016) has also been translated into English.

For Monika

This man was her uncle.

She didn't know what the word meant.

She was six years old.

He bent down to her and explained what was going to happen one last time. Again, she had difficulty understanding him. But she did understand him. She was supposed to repeat something after him. And she did. He gave her a push when the light turned green and she walked across the zebra crossing to the market. She did not look around. He had said she mustn't do that; she had to walk quickly. She walked quickly and kept her eyes on the ground and her hands in her pockets.

She slipped past the men in the passageway between the market stalls without slowing her pace. She kept her head down. The men were setting up their stalls, sweeping, arranging the fruit and vegetables, they moved out of her way or stood still to let her pass. And no one was surprised to see her. That was exactly how it would be, her uncle had said.

It was early in the morning. The street lamps were still lit. The puddles were frozen.

She had eaten nothing since lunchtime the previous day. Bogdan would give her something to eat. Bogdan was a good man. Even if he scolded her, her uncle said, he was a good man. He might scold her to start with, but he would soon stop. And he wouldn't scold her too harshly. She shouldn't say she was hungry. She shouldn't say anything. He would give her something to eat, and it would be better than anything she had eaten in her life.

In the shop, she planted herself in front of the counter and clasped her hands behind her back and said nothing. She looked at the man standing behind the counter.

The man behind the counter is Bogdan, her uncle had told her.

Bogdan asked her what she would like. She didn't reply. Had someone sent her, who had sent her, was she looking for someone, was she waiting for someone. What was her name. How could he help her. She gave no reply.

He let her be.

He fetched sausages, ham, cheese and the dishes of olives, artichokes, courgettes and aubergines preserved in oil from the cold store, and spread the things out beneath the glass countertop.

She did what her uncle had told her. Nothing. She just stood there.

Bogdan cut some bread, laid slices of sausage and cheese on it, cut it into quarters. He lifted her up and sat her on the barstool at the counter. He slid the plate in front of her, poured some yellow juice into a glass.

Her uncle had said she should eat greedily. She

ate the way she always ate. She was more thirsty than hungry. Bogdan refilled her glass. He asked no more questions. When she had finished, he took a bar of chocolate out of a cupboard and gave it to her.

He said: You have to go now.

She looked at him and said nothing. She found it easy to look at him and say nothing. She wasn't afraid of this man.

You have to go now, he said again. You can come back tomorrow. But you have to go now. He lifted her off the stool. She took two steps back into the corner by the umbrella stand, clasped her hands behind her back and went on staring at him.

Look, he said, it's no good, you have to go.

So go!

She said nothing.

You're in the way there, he said. You need to be gone by the time the first customers come in. Do you understand what I'm saying? Do you speak my language? Don't you have any gloves?

She didn't move.

Bogdan stopped worrying about her. When he cut himself a piece of sausage, because that was how he took his breakfast, he passed her a piece as well. Or a pickled gherkin. He brewed some tea and placed two cups on the counter. And finally he lifted her back onto the barstool.

The first customer was the owner of the fishmonger's just up from Bogdan's shop. His hands were red, frozen from scooping ice. He asked who the child was. Was she Bogdan's. That wasn't a serious question.

She came to me, said Bogdan.

He passed the man his milky coffee over the counter, and a plate of bread, sausage, cheese and hummus. Only when the man had finished his coffee and his meal did he ask: How do you mean? And he asked the child: Who are you? What's your name?

She doesn't talk, said Bogdan. Someone will come and fetch her soon. I'm sure someone will fetch her soon.

What do you mean, came to you? asked the man.

I think someone's parked her here, said Bogdan. Her father, maybe, or perhaps she has an older brother. Because it's cold outside and she's in the way, what do I know. He's got business to take care of and doesn't know what to do with her. It's a good idea, if you ask me. I hope word doesn't get around. I'm not cut out for running a kindergarten. But she's sweet, don't you think? Look at her!

The man chewed and looked at her. He held the bread and hummus in front of her mouth. She was full.

What will you do if no one comes to fetch her? he asked.

I'll think about that this evening, said Bogdan.

Send her over to me. For lunch, said the other man. I'll give her something, too.

I'll do that, said Bogdan.

Then the man said some other things, and finally he said: You have to call the police.

The child screamed.

That was something her uncle had drummed into her. She had to pay close attention to the words. When someone said a word that sounded like police, she should scream. He made her repeat the word over and over. He said it to her. He dressed it up in different sentences. He said it casually. He said it very slowly. He mumbled it. Until she understood. She should scream until she had no breath left, and then do the same again, and then stop. She didn't ask what would happen then.

Nothing happened. But the man left Bogdan's shop.

Bogdan picked her up. He smiled at her. She didn't smile back. She stared at him intently. Her hands were cold. He carried her to the back of the shop where the electric heater was. He sat her in an armchair, put his parka round her, wrapped her hands and feet in the padded lining, pulled the hood up over her hair.

A woman came into the shop. She was wearing a fur hat and pulling a shopping trolley. She didn't notice the child. She wanted a special kind of cheese, she couldn't think of the name, she pointed to it. The next customer didn't notice the child, either. Eventually she started singing. Bogdan's shop was full of people – it was lunchtime. Some of them smiled at her, some didn't even look, and others looked over, but absent-mindedly and without smiling. No one asked any questions. Bogdan felt reassured.

But still he waited for the fishmonger to come and fetch the child for lunch.

He came. A little later than promised. It was dark in Bogdan's shop, and at the back, where the child was sitting by the heater, it was even darker, and the sun was now shining outside, so the fishmonger had to accustom his eyes to the darkness.

Has she gone? he asked.

Then he spotted her. He pulled her hood down, cautiously. When she recognised him, she screamed. She screamed until Bogdan picked her up.

The fishmonger said again: You have to call the police, Bogdan.

She screamed.

When she had calmed down, the fishmonger said: Shall I call the hmhm? Someone has to. Otherwise you're going to get yourself in trouble, Bogdan, I'd be careful if I were you.

Let's wait a bit, said Bogdan. Come back this evening. If she's still here, you can call the hmhm. Or I'll call them. Come over, anyway. If the hmhm come, I'd like you to be there.

The fishmonger reached out a hand to the child, who was still in Bogdan's arms, pressing herself against him. This time she didn't scream.

That evening she was gone. She had slipped out of the back door and run away, just like her uncle had told her. Her uncle was waiting for her, where he'd said he would be. He had walked past the shop and whistled with his fingers in his mouth. No one noticed. People often whistled in the market. But she noticed. Her uncle took her by the hand, and they got into the minibus where the other men were waiting.

The next morning she appeared in Bogdan's shop again.

So it went on for several days. In the morning she was there; in the evening she was gone. Bogdan got used to her. And he didn't follow her, either. When his day was over, he would pretend he had something to do in the passageway in front of his shop. To give her a chance to escape through the back door. He didn't want her to be afraid that he might catch her and keep her there.

If anyone asked, he said the child was his niece.

His sister was visiting, he said; she had found a short-term job in the city, and he was temporarily looking after the child. If anyone asked what the child was called, he said Evgenia. The fishmonger warned him again and again that it was risky and there were bound to be consequences. There were sympathetic people in the hmhm, to whom he could confide all of this. Something very dodgy was going on here, he was sure, and Bogdan might be making himself an accomplice to it. But soon he stopped saying things like that. And soon the child stopped screaming when she saw him. Soon she even let him pick her up. Soon she started laughing at him the same way she laughed at Bogdan. She talked, too. But neither Bogdan nor the fishmonger understood her. They had no idea what language she was speaking.

She came in the morning and left in the evening.

Bogdan gave her some padded gloves and a padded hat with ear flaps and some little toys. Her favourite was a bus with children's faces painted in the windows. The fishmonger brought her a coat he said his daughter had grown out of. A good, padded coat.

Her uncle was looking out for her. She had listened as the men talked about her in the place where they slept. She understood when her uncle said: she has to get herself through the winter. She understood that her uncle was looking out for her and that he was doing it reluctantly. The others were reluctant, too. But they still did it. She was given the softest sheets, the thickest blankets, and bananas. The men didn't talk to her. Only her uncle talked to her. The men nodded at her. She thought that meant she was doing everything right. She was glad of that. She didn't have to do anything, and still she was doing everything right.

And then one evening her uncle wasn't where he had said he would be.

She waited, like he had told her to. She put on her mittens, pulled the hat down over her ears and folded her arms. She drew in her chin, because a patch of bare throat was peeping out above her collar. She stood with her back to the wind. People walked past her, but no one said anything. She didn't look like she was lost. She looked like she was waiting. And that was what she was doing. She could see the market stalls, and Bogdan's shop. She saw the lights go off in Bogdan's shop. Then the lights went off in all the market's stalls and shops.

She was cold. She wasn't hungry.

She folded her arms, raised them up to her chin. When everything she saw and heard began to feel unfamiliar, she rubbed her lips together. That was a habit. It had happened quite often before, that everything she saw and heard felt unfamiliar. She rubbed her lips together so hard it made them sore and they started to burn.

She was standing at a crossing. She watched the lights, scanned the people waiting on the other side of the street. Was there anyone who looked like her uncle. She searched for a bobble hat. The cars had happy people in them. The street lamps shone into the cars when they stopped at the lights. It was warm in a car. She didn't see anyone in a car wearing a hat or gloves.

A woman stopped, bent down to her. Said something. She didn't know if it was a question. The woman's mouth was painted. The woman smelled of soap.

She turned her head away. Then she turned round completely. Hunched over. Stayed like that. When she looked over her shoulder, the woman had walked on.

Eventually she started to move. Walked in the direction she thought she had come from with her uncle that first day. But it had been morning then, and now it was evening. The streets all looked the same now, and different from the morning. They were bright with headlights and street lamps, and the sky overhead was dark, as if there were no sky at all.

With her uncle, holding his hand, she had not come along the wide road that the cars were driving down. She remembered walking under a narrow archway before they reached the road. She couldn't find the archway. She turned into a side street and soon found herself on another wide road with lots of cars. She walked a little way along the pavement, past the shop windows, and came to a pedestrian crossing. People were standing there, waiting for the light to turn green. She waited with them. The people crossed the road, and she followed them. She walked after the people, and as they dispersed, she walked after other people. Sometimes just one. If he walked too fast, she waited for the next one. She didn't speak to anybody. She walked as fast as she could, and soon she wasn't cold any more. After a while, there was no one else in sight. Then she stopped, and didn't move until she began to get cold again.

She turned round. But she couldn't find her way back to the market.

She walked past a church. She didn't know what a church was, but she had seen churches before. She was very tired now. It hurt to straighten her knees. Her head was heavy, and there was a pain in her back. She climbed the steps. She wanted to find a gap, to get into the big house. The door made her afraid. The latch was so high up she couldn't see it. When she looked up it was as if the black portal was looming out, threatening to cover her. She was hungry again now, too. She would have loved some of the white bread from Bogdan's shop, preferably just the white bread on its own, with no sausage and no cheese. She decided to stuff some into her pockets the next day. Bogdan had heated up some milk for her – that had been good, too. She sat down on the steps, pulled her gloved hands back into her sleeves, laid the side of her face on her knees and nodded off.

She woke up because she had toppled sideways, and perhaps also because the church clock was chiming. She had never heard anything like it – it made her want to hide. She bounded down the steps and ran towards the trees that grew along the side of the church. Their leafless crowns dissolved into the dark sky.

Between the trees, against the church wall, was a dumpster. She knew what a dumpster was for, even though she didn't know the word for it. Several times she had been out with the women at night and they had fished good things out of dumpsters. The women had pushed back the lid and lifted her up, and she had jumped in. Then the women had shone the torch inside and whispered and praised her, and she had fished out the good things, which were then warmed up and eaten at home. She had watched them push the lid back to open the dumpster. It had been quite easy. She could only imagine that good things were to be found in all the dumpsters in the world. The good things were hidden under the bad things, but she knew how to tell good from bad.

She was very hungry, but she was even more tired. She had never known such tiredness. She thought that at any minute her chest would sink down onto her knees, and her head would fall off. There was a gap between the dumpster and the church wall. She crawled into it. It was narrow. She liked that. It felt like she was being held. She fell asleep. When the bells rang again, she didn't wake up. But after midnight she did wake up.

She was freezing. She couldn't feel her hands. At first she wasn't hungry at all, but her hunger soon returned. She braced her legs against the wall and pulled herself up on the dumpster. She tried to push the lid back. She couldn't do it as well as the women had. She gripped the lid handle and pushed against the wall with her feet. A little crack opened up between the lid and the container, and she crawled through it and fell. She fell onto rubbish. It was pitch black in there. She felt around for the good things. She found a banana skin and chewed it. She found a few more things that smelled good and could be bitten. There was a lot of soft stuff in there.

Newspapers and other things. She lay down on them, curling up in her coat. It was warmer in there than it was outside.

She fell asleep and didn't wake up for a long time.

Snowflakes were falling through the little crack onto her face. She opened her eyes and saw a section of sky. It was bright, it was white.

She could hear the sounds of engines and voices. The engine noises got further away; the voices didn't.

She struggled out of the rubbish that she had burrowed into to escape the night's cold in her sleep, and peered out of the crack. She saw a man and a woman standing not far from the dumpster. They were holding a large umbrella. The snow was falling thickly onto the umbrella. The two of them were talking. It sounded as if they liked each other. Finally the man let go of the umbrella, waved to the woman and walked off, taking small steps across the cobbles. She would have liked to know where the man was going, but for that she would have had to climb out of the dumpster. The woman looked over in her direction. She was wearing a very serious expression now; she took a few steps towards the dumpster and stopped, as if she was listening. She couldn't believe what she was seeing – or perhaps she didn't see anything but a dumpster with its lid open a crack, and didn't see a face and didn't see eyes, or didn't believe that it was a face, that those were eyes. She turned around and left. She, too, took small steps down the cobbled slope, with her arms outstretched, as if balancing on a tightrope, the umbrella in one hand, no longer protecting her from the snow.

The child climbed out of the dumpster and cleaned herself up. She took off her hat and gloves and brushed the dirt off them.

Then the child left, too, walking towards where she thought the market was, and Bogdan's shop.

But she couldn't find Bogdan's shop.

It was lunchtime, and she hadn't eaten anything that day. She tried to quench her thirst by brushing the thin snow into a heap and putting it in her mouth. But that just made her thirstier.

She came across a man sitting on a wall. He had a can of beer in one hand and a cigarette in the other. She didn't say anything; she just pointed at the can. She tapped the can with her finger, and in her language she said: Give me!

That's beer, said the man. You're too little for beer. Go away!

She prodded the can harder. Some beer spilled out.

Give me, she cried out tearfully. Give me!

Alright, I'll get you something to drink, said the man. Stop that! Wait here.

Give me! she screamed in her language and prodded the can.

Fine, come with me then, said the man, and took her by the hand. You stink, he said. My God, you stink to high heaven! Where's your mother? Has someone sent you out begging? Where's your father? Do you even have a father?

Give me, she said, give me. But now when she said it, it sounded like something that wasn't urgent.

The man took her to a supermarket. He didn't let go of her hand. His own hand was clamped tightly around it. Sometimes he tugged at her hand. There was no reason for him to do that. He talked to her. She didn't understand him. When he looked at her, she nodded vigorously. He put two cans of lemonade and two cans of beer into the basket. They went past the bakery section, and the man put a bread roll in with the lemonade and the beer. He paid with a note. Outside, he gave the lemonade and the bread to the child. She ran away at once.

She ran for a good while before looking back. She couldn't see the man. She didn't think he would come after her now. She hid the bread and the lemonade inside her coat and started walking, staying close to the walls of the buildings. She was on a busy road with wide pavements on either side. The pavements were full of people, and nothing looked familiar. It had stopped snowing; the umbrellas weren't up any more. There was a long row of shops. And although it was a bright, white day – brighter and whiter than usual because there was snow on the ground – the brightest lights of all were shining in the shops, and some of the shop windows glinted and glittered in every colour of the rainbow. The doors were open and she could hear music. It was all very confusing.

She looked around for an entryway to sneak into, so she could eat and drink in darkness and silence. She was afraid someone might take the good things away from her. But then she couldn't wait any longer and opened the lemonade in the way her uncle and the women had taught her, and drank from the can right there on the pavement and bit into the roll and drank more lemonade and bit into the roll again. She put the empty can in one coat pocket, and the full one in the other. She held the half roll with both hands.

For a while she was happy, and she stopped thinking about her uncle and the women, and Bogdan and his shop.

The child passed a coffeehouse just as a man and a woman walked out. He held the door open out of politeness, and the woman thanked him.

Hot air streamed out of the entrance. It felt so good to the child. There was a second door inside, and it was only this one that opened into the coffeehouse; the vestibule between was heated so that the customers weren't troubled by a cold draught. She slipped inside quickly, before the door closed, and ducked down into a corner. The waiters inside couldn't see her. Perhaps they would have let the girl sit in the hot space. Perhaps not. There were heaters fixed to the ceiling, glowing and heating the little room. The customers took no notice of the child as they went in and out – some didn't see her at all. She wasn't begging. She was just sitting there. She sat there drinking from a can of lemonade and pulling little pieces off a bread roll. And not looking at anyone. When she had finished eating and drinking, she did nothing. She just sat there, her arms folded over her coat. After a little while the child got too hot, and took off the coat the fishmonger had given her. She had already taken off the hat and gloves. She packed the coat into the corner, lay down on it and fell asleep.

A customer picked the child up and carried her into the coffeehouse.

I don't know what's wrong with her, he said. She's boiling hot.

The owner of the coffeehouse bedded the child down on the carpet in his office and called the police.

The child slept. The coffeehouse owner watched her.

When the child woke up, a woman in police uniform was kneeling in front of her. She had stroked the girl's cheek with the back of her hand.

What's your name? she asked.

The child didn't reply.

Where's your mother?

The officer smelled the child's clothes and pulled a face.

Does she have any papers on her? Anything written?

The coffeehouse owner said the child had had a coat,

a hat and gloves on her. They stink to high heaven, he said. I put them in the storeroom. What shall I do with them?

Did you search the pockets?

No, I didn't.

Bring them here: I'll search through them. Can you get rid of them? asked the officer.

Should I? I mean, they belong to her, said the coffeehouse owner.

She'll get new ones where we're taking her, said the officer. We've got a blanket in the car.

Now the child was just wearing her vest and knickers, with a thin jumper over the top. The officer checked the coat, smelled it and handed it over to be disposed of. She took the child by the wrist and led her out onto the street, where her colleague was waiting in the police car.

It was snowing even harder now, and it was starting to get dark. Another day had passed.

She had been in a car many times in her life. She had liked it. It had been noisy and cramped. Mostly she had sat on someone's lap. Often, they had teased her. In the police car, she was given her own seat. They put a seat belt on her. She didn't know it was a police car. She didn't know it was a seat belt. And she didn't know that the man and the woman were police officers. She had never seen a police officer in her life. She just knew the word. Once some police officers had come by, and her uncle had put his hand over her eyes and a finger on her lips. Afterwards he told her it had been the police. Now, she wasn't thinking anything at all. Her breathing was shallow and fast and she didn't move, not even her eyes.

The male officer sat in the front and drove, and the female officer sat in the back beside the child. She had wrapped her in a blanket. She held a bottle of mineral water to the child's lips so she wouldn't have to take her hands out from under the blanket. The water ran down the child's chin and throat onto her chest.

She liked that. She was feeling hot. She wasn't thirsty. It had been hot in the vestibule of the coffeehouse and in the coffeehouse owner's office, and the blanket was hot, too, and she was wrapped up so tightly she couldn't move. The officer was wearing a little chain around her wrist. She would have liked to have it. There was a little tag on the chain. The officer's face didn't seem friendly to her. Particularly not when she laughed. Not even when she gave the child a bite of a chocolate bar. She only bit off a small piece, and spat it straight out again. She hadn't eaten Bogdan's chocolate, either. She had left it lying on the counter, and the next day it had been gone. She didn't like the way chocolate smelled, and she didn't like the colour, or the fact that it was hard like wood.

The officer wiped the saliva-smeared chocolate off the blanket. She opened the window and threw the tissue out. After that, she left the child alone and just looked straight ahead.

Before they reached their destination, the child had fallen asleep.

A nurse washed the child. First she washed her hair and hands and face, and then she put her in the bathtub and soaped her from head to toe. She even washed her hair a second time. She complimented her on her hair. She had been told that the child didn't speak her language, so she found it easy to say nice things. She complimented her eyes as well. The child's hair reached a long way down her back. She combed her hair carefully. The child stayed calm and didn't complain.

Lastly, the nurse dried the child's thin body with a towel. She took some hand cream out of her handbag – she always had it with her because her hands were so sensitive and she bathed so many children every day. She rubbed the cream into the child's face. It made the child laugh as though she had been tickled. She rubbed cream into her chest and back, and her arms and legs.

Do you want to do your hands yourself? she asked.

She took one of the child's fingers and dipped it into the white cream and showed her how to knead one hand with the other.

The child liked that.

Already, the nurse knew this child was going to be her favourite. She wrapped her in the towel and picked her up. She kissed her head. The child was completely calm.

The nurse could have handed the child over at the clothing issue room; it wasn't her job to take care of her after that. But this child was naked. Her clothes hadn't been sent to the laundry; they had been thrown away. She didn't want to leave the child alone, wearing only a towel, at the door to the clothing room. She wanted to make sure her favourite was given nice things to wear.

There were new cloths and second-hand clothes. The nurse insisted on new. She picked out two pairs of knickers, two t-shirts, two pairs of tights, two pairs of thick socks, two boys' flannel shirts, a Goretex sweat-shirt with a zip down the front, a pair of padded dun-garees, gloves, a hat and a hooded anorak. Washing things and bedding as well. She dressed the child then and there.

The clothing room woman watched her.

The child hid behind the nurse, and the nurse acted as a screen while the child took off the towel.

The nurse led the child into the dormitory and pointed out a bed. She helped her put the sheets on, but made sure the child did most of it herself. There was a little cupboard beside the bed. That was where the child's things should go. The nurse showed her.

There were twenty beds in the dormitory. They stood head to head, foot to foot, in two rows. Only six of the beds were made up. A teddy bear was sitting on each of the made beds. There were no other children in the room. The windows were barred.

The others are having supper, said the nurse. I'll take you to them. Shall I come and have a bowl of soup with you?

But before that, she gave the child the teddy bear that each child received when they were admitted.

Whatever happens, you can keep that, said the nurse. We can write your name on his tag. What's your name?

She pointed to her chest and said loudly: Agnes. Me. Agnes. Agnes. Then she pointed at the girl's chest. Who are you? Me, Agnes, who you? Me, Agnes, who you?

She wasn't angry with the child when she didn't answer.

The dining hall was one floor down, in the basement. A good smell was coming from down there. The girl had an appetite. And now the nurse did, too.

It was a long time since the child had eaten anything hot.

There was broccoli soup and white bread. The way the child ate the soup made the nurse think it was a long time since she'd eaten anything hot. She had a word with one of the women in the kitchen and asked her if there was anything left over from lunch, which had been meat with multi-coloured rice and a blancmange with raspberry sauce. She asked if they could heat up some of the meat and rice. The girl drank a lot as well. She preferred plain water to lemonade.

She wolfed down the rice and meat and it made her throw up. She vomited on the floor and hurriedly wiped her mouth, knocking over her glass in the process and breaking it – she reached for it, cut herself on a shard of glass and then sat mutely, staring into space.

Her right thumb was bleeding.

First the other children stopped talking, then they laughed. There were six of them. They shouted out scornful remarks in their own languages. She didn't understand the languages or the scorn.

But then she did understand something.

We don't need kids who throw up here, a boy shouted. He was fourteen already. He was a big boy. He was wearing a tracksuit, like the others. But his was red. The others' were blue.

I don't want to do it again, she shouted back.

What's your name, he shouted.

I'm not telling, she shouted.

Do I know your mother? Do I know your father?

I'm not telling, she shouted.

Tell me your father's name!

No, she shouted.

Don't you have one?

I'm not telling, she shouted.

The big boy came over. He walked slowly, looking at the nurse and not the child. He was very thin, with a fuzz of hair on his cheeks and his upper lip. He let out a little laugh, and the child saw that he wasn't being mean.

And what's your name? the child asked.

I'm not telling, either, he said.

Is she going to do something to me now? the child asked. She meant the nurse.

When it gets dark, she'll eat you up, said the big boy, deliberately not laughing.

That's not true, said the child. She didn't dare move her eyes to look at the nurse.

The nurse shooed him away with a wave of her hand. She wrapped a tissue round the child's thumb, made the child's right hand into a fist with the thumb tucked inside, and squeezed it.

Hold it, she said, hold it tight! Hold it like this, like this. Tight. This is tight. Hold it tight!

She hurried into the kitchen, got them to give her a roll of sticking plaster and some scissors. She bandaged the cut and wiped the blood off the table.

I was just teasing, the big boy called over, she won't do anything – no one's going to do anything to you. If someone does something to you, you tell me. Then I'll do something to them. Want me to look after you?

The child nodded.

But the nurse thought the big boy had been mean to her favourite. She came over and yanked him to his feet and dragged him by the collar to the table where her favourite was sitting.

Do you know her? she barked at him. She didn't let

him go; she even gave him a shake. Who is she? What's her name? You two know each other, don't you?

No! No, we don't, said the big boy, and he opened his mouth as if he was trying to show he wasn't hiding anything there. He shoved the nurse and shook himself free of her grasp and ran up the stairs out of the dining hall. He swore as he went.

The child understood him. It was a swearword she knew, because her uncle had said it a lot. But her uncle had never meant it nastily, and so the child wasn't frightened by the swearword, even if it sounded nasty. But now she did feel frightened of the nurse.

The nurse wiped the vomit off the floor. The child didn't watch her. She sat there, her fingers laced together, not daring to move her eyes.

In the dormitory the nurse showed her how to brush her teeth. But she already knew how to brush her teeth. She knew what a toothbrush was and what toothpaste was. The nurse brushed too hard, and it hurt. But she didn't cry.

When all the children were in bed, the nurse turned out the light.

Because the nurse had been holding her head still while she brushed her teeth, she hadn't been able to see if the big boy was in the dormitory, too. She could have called out to him now, in the dark. She knew he spoke her language. She thought he was the only one who spoke her language. She would have liked to talk to him. It was so long since she had talked to anyone. The big boy might have teased her then. In fact, she was sure he would. But she didn't dare call out to him. She thought she could see the glint of the nurse's apron by the door.

She pulled the covers over her head, only leaving a gap for her nose and mouth. It was warm and soft. And it was quiet.

The big boy woke her. He whispered in her ear. Don't be scared, kid, he whispered. Do you want to go with us. I know my way round. I know something good.

She opened her eyes and sat up. She saw the big boy, wearing a coat, kneeling beside her bed, and he had a hat on, pulled low over his forehead. It was possible that she was dreaming. She dreamed every night, and she liked dreaming, because the dreams were always nice, and often when she woke up she would think it hadn't been a dream at all, but had really happened, and she would look forward to the daytime when things would carry on like that.

There was another boy standing at the foot of her bed, smaller than the big boy. She couldn't remember seeing him in the dining hall. But in the dining hall they had all been wearing t-shirts and jogging bottoms and they had all looked the same, except for the big boy. And now the smaller one was wearing a coat and hat and gloves as well, and he had a rucksack on his back. His hat, too, was pulled down over his face, a good hat, fur-lined, with long flaps to stop his ears getting cold. She couldn't see much of his face, but she could see that he had thick eyebrows. He came closer to her now, looked her in the eye. He nodded, like adults do when they want to greet each other, but without saying anything.

He reached into his pocket and took something out. It was a thimble; it was made of brass and looked like gold. He held it up to the girl's face, moved it back and forth, now in front of one eye, now the other, slowly. He took the girl's hand and put the thimble on the thumb with the plaster over it and pushed it down. The girl hid the thumb and the thimble in her fist.

Do you want to come with us? the big boy asked.

She nodded.

Then get dressed! But quietly. And don't cough!

She didn't dare ask questions. Tentatively, she climbed out of bed and stood before the big boy in her knickers and t-shirt, barefoot. The big boy had already taken her clothes out of the cupboard. He helped her put them on. Two of everything. He told her to carry her shoes.

Don't say a word, the big boy said again, and don't cough!

They crept across the dormitory. The big boy was leading them not to the entrance door, but to one of the narrow doors in the opposite wall. Behind one door was the washroom, with the trough in the middle and the towels hanging on the walls, and the shelf above for tooth mugs and soap. This door was half open.

The beds in the back part of the dormitory were not occupied. That was lucky for them.

The other door was locked – but the big boy had a key. It wasn't really a key; it was a piece of wire bent into shape. He fiddled with the lock, not very skilfully, and it made a noise and took some time before he had finally unlocked the door. She and the smaller boy stood close to the big boy and watched. They looked at each other, too. But they were wary of saying anything or coughing. She thought the little boy was just as scared as she was. Perhaps even more so.

It was a storeroom for brooms and cleaning products. There was a small window just below the ceiling. It wasn't barred. The big boy shut the door behind him and put the lock pick in his trouser pocket. You would have to be very thin to climb out of the window. It was cramped in the room, and dark.

The big boy pulled a crate over to the wall, opened the window and lifted the child up.

Legs first, he said softly, otherwise you'll fall on your head. He pushed her legs through the window. He didn't know what was on the other side. Just let yourself drop, he whispered in her ear.

Nothing's going to happen to you, he said. Don't be scared. Tuck your chin in, put your hands over your head. Then move to one side and wait for us.

She didn't reply. She stiffened her whole body so it was easier for the big boy to push her through the window. When most of her was through, and her arms and head were the only things still sticking out into the room, where there was no light at all now, since she was blocking the whole window, she did get scared after all, and she whimpered. The big boy shushed her and gave her a shove.

She fell.

She fell into the bushes.

The big boy pulled himself up on the window frame and stuck his head out.

Is everything alright? he asked. Hey, kid, is everything alright? Are you okay?

She nodded. A street lamp shed a thin light over her, and the big boy could see she was nodding.

Then he helped his friend. His friend was scared and whimpered, too. When he was outside and had climbed out of the bushes, he looked around for the child and took her by the hand. They stood like that, waiting for the big boy. They waited a long time. There was no one there to help him. First he tried putting his legs out. But he couldn't do it that way. Going head-first didn't work, either, because then his arms got jammed in the window frame and he couldn't use them to push himself forward. Arms first was his final attempt. The girl and his friend took his hands and pulled.

They ran into the night, the boy's friend and the girl behind the big boy. It wasn't snowing any more, but a biting wind swept around the corners and down the alleyways, hitting their faces like needles. The sky was clear. If they'd looked up, they would have seen the stars. It was very cold. Lifting your head meant your neck would freeze. It was easy to slip and fall on the paving stones and they had to take care. It was still many hours until sunrise.

There was bread and lemonade and bananas in his friend's rucksack. His friend had stolen them, and he had stolen a blanket, too. The big boy explained all this to the girl. The big boy knew his way around. He led them to a metro station. He spoke to his friend in a language the girl didn't understand. Then he spoke to the girl, and his friend didn't understand.

Stay close to me, he told the girl. If you want, you can hold onto me.

He led the way down the steps into the station, walking quickly, scanning the walls and the ceiling for cameras. He stopped behind a pillar and pulled the others close to him.

Breakfast, he said in his friend's language.

Breakfast, he said in the girl's language.

They ate and drank, and the big boy told the girl what he had already told his friend, about this house he knew of – okay, he'd never seen the house for himself, but he knew everything about it. They were on their way to this house, which was empty over the winter and had a freezer full of good things and automatic heating and a television and a computer and the internet. He spoke with his mouth full. The girl listened and believed him.

They stuck close together on the platform. They were the only people there. The big boy kept looking around, he was restless, he explained that children who were on their own got picked up and taken away. He knew that was how it was, but he didn't know why. Three children together, on the other hand, didn't look so suspicious. People went after children who were on their own. Three children were like a family.

They had eaten all the bread and drunk all the lemonade. The big boy had to say everything twice. It wasn't good that they had eaten everything already, he said, first to his friend, then to the girl. Now he would have to think of something else. In two or three hours they would be hungry again. They should at least have left some lemonade. But he wasn't cross – after all, he had eaten and drunk no less than his friend and the girl. The girl had crumbs in her hood, and her lips were sticky from the lemonade. The big boy had brought a packet of tissues. He tore a tissue in half, put one half back in the packet and spat on the other and rubbed the girl's mouth and chin with it. The girl tilted her face up to him and squeezed her eyes shut. He brushed the crumbs out of her hood with his hand.

Can you read? he asked the girl.

She shook her head.

The girl clung to the big boy's sleeve. He put an arm round her shoulders. His friend was standing a short distance away. He pulled his hood even tighter around his face. Now you couldn't see his eyebrows any more. He didn't talk. He nodded or shook his head. He had a five Euro note. He showed the girl and grinned.

The big boy grinned too. Then his friend came over to them and stood with them, one side touching the girl, and the other touching the big boy.

That's his, said the big boy, that's his. He won't give it away, it belongs to him.

And he said the same in his friend's language. His friend nodded. But all the same he put the note in the girl's hand. To let her feel it. Then he took it back and put it away.

The big boy put his other arm around his friend. The metro train pulled in. It pushed a wave of cold air along in front of it. Their hoods flapped. The big boy knew it looked more innocent if a fourteen-year-old had his arms round the shoulders of two younger children than if three children were standing there separately. But he didn't know why that was.

On the train the three of them sat in a row, the big boy in the middle. He put his arms round his friend and the girl again. At the next station two men got on. At the station after that it was a dozen people.

Where are we going? the girl asked.

It was the first thing she had said to the big boy. And she whispered it so quietly that the big boy didn't hear.

His friend said something in his language. Then the girl didn't dare repeat what she wanted to know. A woman sat down opposite them. She didn't have to do that. There were plenty of other seats. But the woman wanted to take a good look at the three of them. She was wearing a large fur hat. The boy's friend turned to him and pressed his face against his upper arm.

When I run, you run after me, said the big boy. In one language, and then in the other.

At the next station a lot of people got on. They were wearing coats and hats and gloves. The big boy bided his time. Just before the train door closed, he leapt up and ran out onto the platform, his friend close behind him.

But the girl didn't follow. She had been taken by surprise and forgot that she was supposed to run after the big boy. And by the time she slid off the seat it was too late. The door closed and the train moved off.

The woman was still staring right at her. She didn't say anything. She didn't smile. She didn't grin. She didn't engage with her at all. She was tired.

The girl was clever. The big boy had promised to look after her. There was no reason to doubt his promise. At the next station she got out. She pretended she was going with the other people, but she just walked in a circle and came back onto the platform. She waited there. She knew what a metro was, and she knew the next train would be along any minute. And she didn't doubt that the big boy and his friend would be on the next train. She looked at the thimble, pulled it off her thumb, put it back on. And took it off again and tried it on all her other fingers. It was too big for them; it only fitted on her sore thumb, because of the plaster.

The big boy and his friend were on the next train. The big boy was clever, too.

She got on and sat down beside them, and everything was as it had been a few minutes ago, before she had lost them. The big boy put his arm around his friend and around the girl. But his eyes were restless again, and he kept turning his head in every direction. The girl fell asleep beside him, her cheek on his thigh.

He didn't wake her.

They stayed on until the final stop. When they left the station, the sky was grey. And it was snowing again. They had reached the outskirts of the city. But it was still a long way to the woods.

The big boy told her about the people who owned the empty house. His friend knew the story. He knew it so well that he nodded and laughed in the right places even though he didn't understand the language the boy was speaking. They were walking through a suburb – the houses were low here and the street lamps were quite far apart. But their light was no longer needed, since the sky was now providing enough of its own.

They passed a bakery, and the big boy interrupted his story.

He said something to his friend. The girl watched the two of them, and she saw the big boy make an angry face. His friend reached into his pocket and gave the big boy the five Euro note.

Wait here, said the big boy, and don't talk to anyone.

He went into the bakery.

The girl saw the tears rolling from the smaller boy's eyes. You had to look closely. You could only see them on his cheeks as they ran the short distance from his eyes to the lower edge of his hood. His mouth was hidden inside the hood. His arms hung at his sides, and he was holding his right glove in his left hand. He looked the girl in the eyes. She didn't move. She stood exactly where the big boy had left her.

After a while the big boy left the bakery. He strode past them, not looking at them, not looking around for them. Gave them no signal. Didn't whisper anything to them. Pretended he was alone. And they were alone too, and had nothing to do with him. He was carrying two paper bags. They ran after him. And when they came to a side street, they had to run even faster: the big boy turned the corner, and now he wasn't walking any more, but running, and now all three of them were running, and the girl was the slowest. The big boy and his friend didn't wait for her. But she wasn't frightened. She could see the two of them running ahead of her, and she saw them disappear down a driveway. Before they disappeared, the big boy waved to her. His hand told her to hurry.

The big boy undid two buttons on his coat. He had two large loaves of bread hidden underneath. He had stolen them from the bakery. There were two sugared doughnuts in his coat pockets – he had stolen them too, and he gave one to the girl and one to his friend. They ate them at once. The big boy took a large bite of each doughnut and sucked out the jam. Icing sugar clung to their lips. The paper bags contained plastic bottles of lemonade. The big boy had paid for those with his friend's five Euro note.

They put the bread and the lemonade in the rucksack. They waited a while longer before setting off. Soon, they had reached the woods. When the buildings had disappeared from view behind them, the big boy carried on with the story of the empty house where they would live over the winter. They were walking slowly now, as if they were out for a stroll and had nothing to fear.

This time they portioned out the food and drink. They passed a stream, there wasn't much water flowing there, the edges were iced over, but the water was clear, and because the girl didn't really like the sweet lemonade, the big boy poured the contents of her bottle into his and his friend's, and filled the girl's bottle with water.

At first the track took them through sparse beech woods, snow lay between the trunks, and snow was falling from the sky, it fell in such thick flakes that they couldn't see from one tree to the next, and the wind was even more biting here than in the city, they lowered their heads to stop the flakes blowing into their eyes. There wasn't a single footprint, and it was silent, apart from the wind howling in their hoods. Their faces burned. They walked and didn't speak. The big boy still hadn't finished his story.

Then they found themselves in a thick pine forest. The track led steeply upwards. They couldn't see the sky any more. The pine branches joined together above the track to form a roof. It wasn't really a track now, but a footpath. It was veined with exposed roots. From time to time the girl slipped and fell. The trees kept the wind out and the snow, too. And to the children, it felt warm in there. They had no sense of how long they had been walking. Only that they were hungry again.

The boy's friend asked something. Or said something. It could be that his voice always sounded like he was asking a question. He had a high voice. Then he started crying. They didn't want to carry on while the boy's friend was crying. So they sat down. But they quickly got up again, because the big boy said there were better places than this.

If he has something to eat, the big boy said to the

girl – as if it was his friend, not she who was the littlest one – if he has something to eat, he'll feel better, you'll see. As if the big boy was the father and the girl was the mother and his friend was the child.

A few paces off into the woods, away from the path, there was a clump of young spruces. The saplings were slight, and so close together and so thick with branches that you couldn't see through them. They crawled inside. The ground was dry and soft, the slender trunks sticky with sap. They huddled together. They bent some of the spiny branches down or plucked the needles off them. It smelled of sap and pine needles. And of the earth their shoes had churned up. The big boy shared out the bread. They ate and didn't speak and drank from their bottles.

His name's Arian, said the big boy. He hugged his friend to him, and his friend laughed. What's yours?

She didn't know her name. Yiza, she said. That's what they had called her. She knew that Yiza wasn't a name.

That's not a name, said the big boy.

But from then on he called her Yiza.

I'm Shamhan, he said.

Shamhan, she said. Arian, she said.

Then they went on eating and didn't speak and drank from their bottles. Yiza tapped the trunk of a tree with the thimble. She tapped, she listened and laughed.

They didn't know what time it was. But they didn't know what day of the week it was, either. The sun didn't come out from behind the clouds, and if it had come out from behind the clouds, the children wouldn't have seen it. They could hear the wind high above them. It made a rustling noise that sounded like they were sitting in a huge room, the ceiling of which had been designed for a giant or a god. Shamhan still hadn't finished the story of the empty house. But Arian wasn't crying any more, and that was good. They got the blanket Arian had stolen from the home out of the rucksack and wrapped it around themselves. Yiza lay between the boys and warmed them and was warmed by them. They fell asleep like that.

They woke in the middle of the night. Yiza was too hot, and Shamhan and Arian were cold. Then Arian lay in the middle, and an hour later they woke up again, and Shamhan lay in the middle. They could have stayed hidden there for a long, long time, and no one would have found them.

Arian was the first to wake. He was lying on the outside. His back was cold, and his legs were cold. He crawled out from under the blanket. Shamhan had his arm round Yiza. Her head was under the blanket, pressed against Shamhan's chest. Arian laid the blanket over her back and wrapped it round her legs. He pulled the drawstrings of his hood tight, knotted them under his chin, pushed the sleeves of his anorak down over his gloves. There wasn't room to stand upright in the little copse. The branches began to grow from the trunks half a metre above the ground at most. You had to crawl. Arian tore off a piece of bread, drank some lemonade and crawled out of the copse.

He could see a shimmer of light through the needle roof of the tall pine trees. It could have been the moon. Or the morning. Arian climbed up the slope, sometimes crawling on all fours because the slope was so steep and his shoes kept slipping. He turned round again and again. He didn't want to lose sight of the little copse. And if Shamhan or Yiza called out to him, he wanted to hear them. He didn't know what he was expecting to find up on the track. Perhaps he just wanted to make sure the track was still there. Even if it was just a footpath and not a proper track, people had still walked down it before him, and he wanted to make sure.

He rested. He could feel his heart thumping in his throat. He couldn't see very far in the darkness. He couldn't see the little copse any more. But it was only a few metres away. He wouldn't even have to shout. If he spoke in a normal voice, Shamhan and Yiza would hear him. And if he shouted to them, they would wake up.

He sat down on the root of a spruce. When he couldn't feel his heart any more, he went on climbing.

It had snowed through the night, and the snow had slipped through the pine-needle roof and covered the path. Arian didn't know where he was any more.

He picked up some snow and put it in his mouth. He had lost his piece of bread. It was so quiet that he was afraid of the rushing sound in his ears. He thought he could hear the blood whistling through the veins in his throat. A tree trunk creaked. Then it was silent again. The sound of an engine, a long way off. A lorry. Arian knew what lorries sounded like.

He sat down again.

He whispered: No.

He waited for an answer, then he whispered: Oh, right. Yes. Why?

And waited for an answer again.

He didn't believe that Shamhan would punish him. He won't do it, so that Yiza won't cry. Little children sometimes sit down on the ground and refuse to walk any further. Shamhan knew that and he didn't want it to happen.

Now he wasn't whispering any more, but speaking quietly: That's how I'll do it. I can do it like that, yes.

He unzipped his anorak, pulled down his trousers and pants in one go, and relieved himself. He wiped his bottom with snow and soil. And washed his hands with snow and soil.

He slithered down the slope following his own footprints. He saw the little copse. He paused.

From here to here, he said softly. That's how I'll do it. I can do it. Can I do it like that?

He listened for an answer.

Right, he said, then that's how I'll do it.

He listened.

One here, he said, then one here and one here.

He listened. He nodded.

That's how I'll do it.

And nodded.

He crawled into the copse. Shamhan and Yiza were still asleep. They were lying just as he had left them. We need firewood, he thought. A lighter would be even better. He decided to mention it to Shamhan. He loved fire. He would have liked a cup of tea. There was some tea right at the bottom of the rucksack. He had taken two handfuls of teabags from the bowl at the home and put them in the pockets of his jogging trousers. He had got away with that twice. A lot of cups of tea.

People round here aren't stupid, said Shamhan. Particularly the people who have money, they're not stupid. They go away in winter. They go to Italy. Or Spain. They can walk around in short sleeves there.

Would you do that too, if you were rich? Arian asked.

No, I wouldn't.

Why not?

Because then people would break into my house.

Are we going to break into their house? Arian asked.

Yes, we are. Shamhan translated what Arian had asked and what he had told him.

Why are we doing that? said Yiza.

We'll put the heating on. We'll make some tea. We'll see what's in the freezer. We'll watch TV. Is that good?

Yiza looked over at Arian, and Shamhan translated again.

Arian said: That's good.

He says it's good, said Shamhan.

Then Yiza, too, said: That's good.

What would you like to eat? What's your favourite food?

I don't know what it's called, said Yiza.

And you?

Meat, said Arian.

Do you like watching TV? Shamhan asked.

Yiza nodded.

There's bound to be meat in the freezer, said Shamhan. First he said it in Arian's language, then in Yiza's language, which was his language, too. We can find some. Chicken or lamb. Or both. I'm going to have chicken. I like chicken. I can cook chicken. I've cooked chicken before. I fried it in a frying pan. We'll fry the meat in the kitchen. They've got everything there. We can make some rice to go with it. Or we can have bread. And what do you like to drink?

Lemonade, said Arian.

Milk, said Yiza.

Hot or cold?

Hot, please.
Okay.

They were hungry. And so they walked on into the brightening daylight.

But it wasn't a terrible hunger yet. They would just have liked something to eat, and there was a sticky, bitter taste in their mouths.

They turned round and went back to the road. It was snowing, but it was warmer now, and the snow was mixed with rain. They had been given proper shoes in the home, but they weren't made for a whole morning walking through slush. Water sloshed over the sides of their shoes and trickled into their socks.

On the road, Shamhan didn't dare go in the direction they had come from the previous day. He thought someone might have discovered his theft from the bakery. He thought the shop girl might be on the alert, looking out of the window, and would recognise him and call the police. They walked one behind the other. Arian behind Yiza behind Shamhan. But in this direction, it was a long way to the next village. And you could only get something to eat where people lived. And you could only get a lighter or matches where people lived, too.

The blood was throbbing in Yiza's thumb. She pulled off the thimble and picked up some snow and pressed her thumb into the snow. The plaster was dirty and sodden. She put the thimble back over it.

Sometimes a car sounded its horn. Sometimes a car stopped. Then they ran off into the fields and didn't look back. And kept running until they heard the engine start up again. The cars had their headlights on even though it was daytime. The day had never got properly light. It was raining. Shamhan's and Arian's jackets and Yiza's coat were soaked through, and their hoods were soaked through, too. Arian was crying again. Yiza was crying as well now. It was mid-afternoon and the sky was already growing dark.

Is it much further? Arian asked.

I don't know exactly, said Shamhan.

Yiza asked if it was much further as well.

He replied: It's not much further now, sweetie. You'll sleep well tonight.

I slept well yesterday, too, said Yiza.

No you didn't, said Shamhan. You kept waking up. Have you forgotten?

I forgot about that, said Yiza.

Where did we sleep? Shamhan asked her. Tell me! Where did we sleep?

I don't remember, said Yiza.

Where did we sleep last night? he asked Arian. Do you know?

In the woods, said Arian.

She doesn't remember that, said Shamhan in Arian's language.

There were crows overhead. Not directly above

them. They were flying over the field to their left. But they were following the three walkers.

A dozen hay barns were scattered across a large, snow-covered field. They took shelter from the rain in the first of them. There was a padlock on the door, but it wasn't fastened. They were wet through. They didn't talk about hunger.

The hay barn had a loft that came halfway out into the room. The walls and the roof were solid. The floor was made of rammed earth, swept clean. Hay forks and drying racks leant against the wall. A ladder led up to the loft. They climbed up one after another, Shamhan going last. He pulled the ladder up behind him.

Some of the hay had been compressed into bales, and some was loose. The floor was dry and dusty. That's good, said Shamhan, the dust will dry our clothes. They stuffed hay into their shoes. They took all their clothes off, turned them inside out and stuffed hay into the sleeves and the trouser legs and spread their pants, vests and socks out on the dusty floor and covered them in dust. Shamhan wrapped Yiza and Arian in the blanket. Then he heaped hay on top of them until they were buried in it. Finally, he crawled through the hay to them and got under the blanket. They clung to each other. They warmed each other. It was better than in the woods. Even though in the woods they'd had bread and lemonade. Here they had nothing. They quickly fell asleep.

In the night, Shamhan got up. He wanted to have a think about something, but had forgotten what it was. He had known it in his dream. He crawled across the wooden boards, feeling his way with his hands. Everything around him was black. It didn't make a difference if his eyes were open or shut. His eyeballs might just as well have been stones. He found the jackets and Yiza's coat and he found Yiza's dungarees and Arian's trousers and his own and he found the shoes as well. He pulled out the damp hay and refilled them with dry hay. He pushed a hay bale right up to their little camp, so that they were hemmed in by two bales. Then he slid back under the blanket. The hay prickled his back, but that didn't bother him. Soon he wasn't cold any more, either. There was no sound. Only the children's breathing close to his ear.

Their things still weren't dry the next morning. Yiza and Arian woke up crying. They wanted something to eat. Stalks clung to their naked bodies, and there was hay in their hair. Their bodies were thin and white. As if they were glowing from inside. Arian was even thinner than Yiza. They shivered, their teeth chattered, they cried, and Shamhan began to cry with them. Then they fell silent. And Shamhan cried alone. Yiza and Arian suddenly weren't hungry any more. Yiza and Arian would have liked to talk to each other. What he thought about this. What she thought. What they *could* think about Shamhan crying. But Arian didn't know a single word of Yiza's language, and Yiza didn't know a single word of Arian's. Shamhan sat on the floor and sobbed and shivered, his teeth chattering, just as they had sobbed and shivered and their teeth had chattered. Now they stood in front of him with their hands behind their backs and shivered in the cold and their teeth knocked together. But sunlight was falling through the tiny glassless window in the gable, just below the roof.

A beam of light with dust dancing in it.

We need to wait until our clothes are dry, said Shamhan. First in Arian's language, then in Yiza's. Otherwise we'll get sick. And we don't have any aspirin.

The sun shone for an hour that morning. They sat huddled together in the hay, naked, wrapped in the blanket, and looked at the sunbeam until it was extinguished and they heard the rain on the barn roof again. It was a heavy rain, driven by a strong wind.

They passed the time by sleeping.

Shamhan kept checking on their clothes. He woke Arian and Yiza. Our vests and pants are dry, he said. We have to beat the dirt out of them, or it will make us sore.

What fun that was! They beat their underwear against the dry wood of the barn wall. Then they chased each other around, each of them hitting the others on their bare backs and heads and their bare arms.

Hunger reminded them. They stayed in the barn

another two days and two nights, then one dark morning it drove them out into the rain; it was pitiless and it made them look pitiless, too. They didn't know where to go, but Shamhan went first and Arian and Yiza followed him, and he walked as if he knew the way, planting his feet firmly with every step, and they followed as if they trusted him.

The sun had not yet risen above the clouds and mist when they reached a place where people lived. There were detached houses with garages and gardens, bungalows with satellite dishes on the roofs and low walls separating them from the street. There was a bus stop opposite the first bungalow. They huddled together beneath the bus-stop roof and peered over at a window where a light was shining.

They saw the light go out, and soon after that they saw a man and a woman leave the house. The woman waited in the driveway, in the rain, holding a flat bag over her head, the man raised the garage door, and soon they were driving off. The house was empty and dark.

Those people won't come back 'til this evening, Shamhan said to Arian. They have jobs. They don't have any children. They both have jobs. And they only have one car. They live alone and they don't know anyone. He takes her to work, and in the evening he picks her up again.

What? said Yiza.

Nothing, said Shamhan.

Nothing, said Arian. It was his first word in Yiza and Shamhan's language.

They ran across the street in the rain, climbed over the little wall, and Yiza and Arian crept along the side of the house after Shamhan, their backs hunched like Shamhan's, their knees bent like Shamhan's. Behind the house they couldn't be seen from the street, and they couldn't be seen from the other houses, either, because the gardens were separated by tall hedges.

The basement windows were each fitted with a vertical iron bar.

Come here, Shamhan said to Yiza. Come here to me. Do you see that? Can you get your head through there? Try! Can you?

She could.

It's a good job we brought you, said Shamhan.

Yiza smiled and showed her pretty teeth and nodded vigorously. And she smiled at Arian and showed him her pretty teeth as well.

What if they come back now? Arian asked.

I've explained this to you already, said Shamhan.

But you can't *know* that. Let's not do it! Please, let's not do it! I'm really scared. Please, let's not do it!

But I want to, said Shamhan. I'm hungry. Aren't you hungry? Yiza and I are hungry.

But what if they do come back after all?

They won't come back.

What if they do?

Then we'll hear them and run away and take some food with us. That's still better, isn't it?

What if we don't hear them?

We'll definitely hear them. They've got a car. We'll definitely hear the car. Then we'll run away and take some food with us.

What if they don't come back in the car?

They've got a car! Why would they come back without the car, when it's raining? Of course they'll come back in the car.

What if the woman comes by herself?

She won't come by herself. It's raining. She doesn't have an umbrella. I didn't see an umbrella.

What if she comes anyway?

Her husband will pick her up from work. That will be in the evening. We'll be long gone. And we'll have taken some food with us.

But it's not the house you told me about. Is it?

No, it isn't.

So that house doesn't exist?

No – it does. But it's not this one.

So we're not going there any more?

No – we *are* going there. But first we're going into this house.

And we're going to stay in the other house all winter?

Yes, in the other one.

Not this one?

Probably not this one, no.

Arian shook his head, looked down at the ground, dragged his shoe across the rotting brown grass.

What? said Shamhan.

Arian shook his head.

What!

Shamhan went to look for a rock in the garden. He had to look for a long time. Yiza and Arian watched him. He didn't dare go too far out into the garden. It was daytime now, it wasn't a bright day, but it was daytime, and someone in the house next door might see him in the garden. He couldn't find a rock. He kicked the windowpane in with his heel. He reached through the hole, felt cautiously for the catch and opened the window. Yiza took off her coat. Like he had told her.

Remember how we did it in the home? said Shamhan. We're going to do that again here, exactly the same.

Yiza nodded. She looked very serious.

He lifted her up, carrying her in his arms like a baby, and pushed her through the window, legs first.

Help me, he said to Arian.

Arian shook his head and turned round and pretended he was keeping a lookout.

Watch out for the broken glass, said Shamhan to Yiza.

Okay, she said.

She slipped her head past the iron bar and then she was in the house.

Okay, she called out.

She padded through the basement and up the short flight of stairs into the house. She found the sitting room and opened the patio door. Like Shamhan had explained to her.

It was warm in the house. There was a radiator in every room, and all the radiators were very warm. They took off their clothes and hung them over the radiators in the sitting room and the bedroom. They leaned their shoes upside down against the heating pipes. Yiza and Arian did what Shamhan told them. They hung their blanket over the radiator in the hall. And the rucksack over the radiator in the kitchen. Shamhan put Yiza under the shower and made hot water rain down on her.

Can I sit down? she asked.

Yes, he said. But don't fall asleep, or you'll drown.

The sitting room was full of dolls. There were dolls on top of the television, on shelves, on the back of the sofa, on the window sills. Dolls with red woollen hair and knitted dolls and dolls made of porcelain and plastic and dolls made of felt. Shamhan gave one of them to Yiza. She played with it as the hot water fell on her. But she didn't know what to play, and when she'd had enough he dried her off and tied two pillows from the bedroom to her with the belt of a dressing gown, one pillow at the front, one at the back. She looked funny; he showed her in the big mirror, and they squealed with laughter. He and Arian wrapped themselves in the duvets from the marital bed, which were filled with down and had white covers on them.

Show me that, said Shamhan.

He took off the thimble and removed the plaster. Her thumb was red and swollen. There was pus in the cut. He squeezed out the pus and wiped it off with toilet paper. He heated some water in a pan and added salt to it. He took Yiza's hand and dipped it into the hot salty water. She screamed, but Shamhan didn't let go. After a while she stopped screaming, and after a little while longer, he didn't have to hold her hand there any more. She sat with the pan on her knees and waited, her hand in the salty water.

Shamhan found plasters and some schnapps. He dried Yiza's thumb, squeezed the last of the pus out of it and poured schnapps over the cut. This time she didn't scream. He stuck a plaster on her thumb and she turned to look at Arian as she put the thimble back on. He nodded solemnly.

Then they sat down in the kitchen and ate.

They ate bread with butter and jam and bread with butter and honey. While they ate, Shamhan filled the rucksack with good things from the fridge. Sausage, cheese, peppers, tomatoes, an opened jar of olives, an opened bottle of white wine, three pots of yoghurt. In the larder he discovered tins of peaches, tins of peeled tomatoes, tins of peas. Arian found some ham at the back of the fridge, wrapped in paper, it didn't smell off.

Arian poured milk into a pan and set it on the hob. He poured the hot milk first into Yiza's cup, then Shamhan's. He put some water on to boil in a second pan. He used it to make tea with the teabags he had stolen from the home. Fruit tea. It smelled good.

Can I have one too? Shamhan asked.

Arian fetched a second cup from the cupboard, dropped a teabag in and poured water over it.

Yiza too? he asked.

You too? asked Shamhan.

Yiza nodded.

Shamhan dried the saucepan and put it in the rucksack with the other things.

Arian searched the cupboards and found boxes of matches and two lighters. And knives, forks and spoons, a tin opener and a bottle opener. He put everything in the rucksack. They didn't find any money. They were very cheerful. There was a radio in the kitchen, and they switched it on and listened to music. Then they fried some eggs, all ten eggs they had found, and fried the ham that didn't smell off, and ate them with bread and butter and tomatoes and bananas. All while they listened to the music. Yiza drank a lot of water and had to keep going to the toilet and she was desperate and didn't make it in time. She was scared Shamhan would tell her off, but he didn't.

When they had finished eating and drinking, they

got into the marital bed. They woke up and ate some more, Shamhan found some beer, he had two bottles and got drunk, and they fell asleep again.

They searched the house and found a rucksack that was bigger than theirs, with a lot of pockets and a zip, and they filled it with all the other things they thought they might need. Two woollen blankets, schnapps from the sitting room, crisps from the sitting room, chocolate biscuits, a fat candle with a name written on it. Three large plastic mineral water bottles.

We're rich, said Shamhan. He was still a little bit drunk.

You're the captain, said Arian, and held out his fist, and Shamhan touched it gently with his own, knuckle to knuckle.

Shamhan picked Yiza up and kissed her. And what do you say I am? he asked her.

Uncle, she said.

What's she saying? Arian asked.

Nothing. Don't worry.

Nothing, said Arian in Yiza and Shamhan's language.

Nothing, Yiza replied.

In the afternoon, when the clouds were growing darker, they left the house. Their clothes were warm and dry. Their bellies were warm and full. Shamhan and Arian were carrying heavy loads. They set off back the way they had come. It was snowing again.

They brushed the snow off their shoulders and hoods. That way their clothes wouldn't get wet. They didn't speak to each other. Yiza dawdled behind the other two. Shamhan had to keep telling her to walk faster. She would so have liked to stay in the house. In the hay barn, they each wrapped themselves in their own blanket. Shamhan took a large swig from the schnapps bottle, then blew out the candle and fell asleep. Yiza was already sleeping. Arian sat up for a while longer.

Should that go there? he whispered into the blackness.

He listened, cocking his head to one side.

Or there? he asked.

He listened.

And nodded.

Then he lay back, pulled the blanket over his head and fell asleep.

It was so easy. The police officers followed the footprints in the snow. They were only vaguely visible now. But they were visible.

They took away their entire haul. They even took away the rucksack from the home. And the teabags. They took away everything except the clothes they were wearing. And the little lighter they hadn't found in Arian's trousers.

They sat in a row in the back of the police van, their backs to the driver, an officer in the seat opposite. They could only see his face when it was lit up by the headlights of the oncoming cars. The window between them and the driver's seat behind them was barred. Arian and Yiza didn't understand the officer's language. They couldn't reply. Shamhan understood the questions, but he pretended not to.

Without looking at Arian and Yiza, he said: Don't talk. Don't look at him. That's best. He said it once in Yiza's language, and then in Arian's. The officers didn't understand either language, and thought they were one and the same.

It sounded like Shamhan was praying. He kept repeating: Don't talk. Don't look at him. That's best. As he spoke he swayed gently back and forth, his eyelids half closed, his head thrown back. The officer believed he was praying.

They were on a wet road, travelling through the countryside. It was night-time. The children sat facing backwards, they saw the red tail lights of the cars that had passed them in the other direction. The officer said nothing. He had given up asking questions. Yiza had fallen asleep. She had toppled sideways, and her head was in Shamhan's lap. He ran one finger across her forehead, into her hair, then down to her mouth and her chin. Once, Shamhan's eyes met the policeman's. The officer smiled. And Shamhan smiled back. And the officer went on smiling, although he didn't attach any meaning to the smile, neither his nor the boy's, and he thought to himself, in his place I'd smile too, I'd think it might make the policeman feel more lenient, and he noticed that Shamhan's smile did make him feel more lenient.

The traffic grew heavier; they were heading into the city. And then they reached the police station. They had to get out. No one touched them. They had to get out.

Get out, please. What's the matter with the girl?

Shamhan picked Yiza up. She whispered in his ear that she was awake, but he mustn't give her away. Shaman said – and now it sounded like he was singing – Don't talk. Don't look at anyone. He said the same thing in Arian's language.

Arian was holding onto Yiza's foot. He had pulled his hood tight again so you couldn't see his eyebrows. He kept glancing up, wanting to look into Shamhan's face and read it. Maybe Shamhan's face would tell him what was going to happen next. But Shamhan just looked straight ahead or up at the sky, from which snowflakes were now falling once more. They fell slowly: fat, heavy flakes that settled on their shoulders.

The officer who had sat opposite them in the van said: There's tea inside. Come inside. He stroked Yiza and asked: Are you asleep? Is she asleep?

Shamhan hugged her tight. No understand, he said. No understand. Secretly, he dug his thumbs into Yiza's side and said quietly in her language, which was also his: You mustn't talk.

The officers walked ahead of them. Yiza whispered in Shamhan's ear: I won't talk.

I'll do all the talking, said Shamhan. First he said it in Yiza's language, then in Arian's.

They were led into a bright, warm room. Police officers in uniform were sitting behind a reception desk. They were directed towards soft seats where they were to wait. We don't know anything about them, said the officer who had sat opposite them in the van.

What's he going on about? asked the officer who had driven the van.

He's praying, said his colleague.

Don't look at me, Arian. And don't say anything. Listen to me. We have to leave Yiza behind. Don't look at her. Don't look at me. They think I'm praying. They mustn't think I'm talking to you. Yiza mustn't think I'm talking to you, either. Close your eyes, pretend you're going to sleep. We're going to be sitting here for a long time. They don't know what language we're speaking. They don't know what kind of interpreter to call. They'll get tired. When they see that we're tired, they'll get tired, too. They're not all that interested in us. We're not important. They'll get careless, because they think we're tired and we're not important. Yiza can't run as fast as you and I can. If we wait for her, they'll catch us. Nothing's going to happen to her. They'll take her back to the home. She'll stay there over winter. They wouldn't let us stay in the home over winter, either of us, Arian. She's everyone's favourite. They all want to stroke her. You've seen it with your own eyes. Everyone feels sorry for her. And everyone loves her. They'll say: let's keep her for one more day, let's keep her one more week, and then they'll get used to her, and then a woman will say: come home with me, don't you want to live with me, and she'll say yes, because she always says yes. She'll be fine whatever happens, but *we* won't, Arian, you and me. She doesn't even know her own name. If you don't know your name, you don't have a mother or a father. Mothers and fathers tell you your name. They keep saying your name, because they like saying it and hearing it. Yiza has no one. They can't deport her. Where would they deport her to? If someone doesn't have a name, then they don't have any relatives. There's no one waiting for her. There's no one to take her in. They'll deport you. And me. I'm not a favourite. You're not a favourite either. When your voice gets deeper, you're not going to be anyone's favourite any more. You've already got eyebrows like a man. We should have run away when we got out of the car. There was a moment when they weren't paying attention. I know you can run fast. I can run fast, too. But we couldn't run away because I was carrying Yiza. That was a mistake. I won't pick her up again. It wasn't good that we took her with us. When I run, you run too. Run in a different direction to me. Run until you can't run any more. We'll meet at the river, where we met before. If you remember where, then cough now. Don't look at Yiza, Arian. If you look at her, it will make you weak. Then you won't run fast enough, and they'll catch you and deport you. Arian. They don't like children who have eyebrows like yours. I know that. You know it too, that's why you hide your eyebrows. Nothing's going to happen to Yiza. She'll do better than us. She's a favourite. I'm not a favourite. And you're not, either.

What god is he praying to? asked the policeman who had driven the van. If we knew that, we might be getting somewhere.

They drank tea and ate sandwiches. One of the policemen wiped Yiza's mouth. She pushed his hand away. She pressed herself against Shamhan. Buried her head in his armpit. They waited. But didn't know what they were waiting for. Shamhan thought they were waiting for an interpreter. The officers had made some phone calls and they were still making phone calls, but they hadn't said the word *interpreter*. When they were on the phone, they laughed into the receiver. Or else Shamhan had missed the word. Or they used a different word for it. Or they were calling about something else. Yiza curled up so that all of her fitted onto the chair, and laid her head on Shamhan's thigh. Arian did the same on the other side.

The officers thought the three of them were siblings. They guessed their ages. The bigger boy might be younger than he looked, they thought. Then they talked about other things. One of them kept going outside to smoke a cigarette, and brought the smell of smoke back in with him. Soon it was quiet in the room. The officers who had brought the big boy and the two little ones in were long gone.

Shamhan now thought the officers would leave them sitting there overnight, and would only fetch an interpreter in the morning, or not fetch one at all and cart them off somewhere without interrogating them. He closed his eyes. He wanted them to think he was sleeping. But he wasn't sleeping.

After midnight, two policemen brought a man in. They were on his left and right, holding him by his upper arms and giving orders. Shamhan couldn't tell who they were giving orders to: the man, or each other. The man was drunk. He had on a heavy, light-coloured coat with a fur collar. It wasn't buttoned, and underneath he was wearing a suit, the jacket open as well, his shirt and tie spattered with dried blood. The man had a very deep voice. Shamhan couldn't understand what he was saying, he wasn't speaking clearly. And Shamhan was only interested in whether the man was talking about them. He didn't think he was. The man hadn't looked at them when he was brought in. He was drunk, but he seemed sensible. His voice was calm and sensible. He took a pair of glasses out of his coat pocket and put them on. Then you couldn't see the anger in his eyes, either. But the two policemen didn't let go of his arms. They stood in front of the desk and held onto him and gave their orders and explained to their colleagues what had happened. Shamhan gave Arian a shove. He sat up at once. Sat up straight. Breathed quickly.

Shamhan carefully pushed Yiza aside. She woke up and immediately wanted to lie back down on his leg. Shamhan didn't let her. She lay down on her other side, resting her head on her arm.

Shamhan squeezed Arian's hand.

Ready, he said.

When the man started yelling and lashing out at the officers, Shamhan leapt up and made for the door. But Arian stayed where he was.

It was a long way to the door, and he had to pass the desk. The man in the heavy coat with the fur collar struggled free from the policemen's grasp, he was yelling even louder now, but without words, and he smashed both fists into Shamhan's head. And Shamhan fell down. The man started kicking him, yelling with every kick. Shamhan shielded his head with his hands and forearms, he rolled to one side, tried to get up, but the man kicked him again, jumped on him with his whole weight and yelled and struck out at the policemen who were trying to pull him off Shamhan. He hit one of the policemen in the eye and blood sprayed onto his uniform. The policeman pulled the cosh out of his belt and hit the man on his back and on the back of his head. The man fell over onto Shamhan, covering him with his big coat.

Yiza had woken up. She stood pale-faced in front of her chair, and Arian stood pale-faced in front of his chair. He took her by the hand and they walked across the room, walked to the door and left the police station and walked into the snowstorm, they held each other's hands and walked and didn't turn around.

Yiza whimpered and kept saying something, but Arian couldn't understand her; he kept saying something, too, but Yiza couldn't understand. They both whimpered, but they didn't stop walking, and they didn't look round, and neither of them let go of the other's hand. It wasn't snowing any more. The street was wet and glittered in the light of the street lamps. The black sky was low above them, they could almost feel it on their heads. But the wind was even harsher now. There weren't many cars around.

Then they couldn't go any further.

Yiza didn't want to walk any more. Arian pulled her along behind him. But she just fell over. She just lay on the pavement. She just fell asleep on the pavement. He picked her up and dragged her a little way. He wasn't very strong. He left her there and carried on walking. But then he turned back and crouched down beside her.

Yiza, he said. Arian, he said. And he said: Nothing. Those were all the words they had in common.

Yiza got up, and they kept walking. But then they really couldn't go any further. Neither of them could go any further. Arian saw a lorry parked on the other side of the road. He knew about lorries. They ran across the road. Arian walked around the lorry, he got up on the footplate and looked into the cab. Yiza waited for him to come back. She slept standing up. The cover over the back of the lorry was secured with straps. Arian undid one of the straps. He lifted Yiza up and she climbed inside, then he followed her. They felt their way forwards in the dark. There was a pile of folded tarpaulins against the wall between the back of the lorry and the cab. They covered themselves with one and fell asleep at once. They lay face to face, giving each other their warm breath. Arian's fingers clutched the lighter in his trouser pocket.

They didn't wake up when the engine started. They didn't wake up when the lorry started to move. Or when it left the city. The sun rose into a cold, cloudless sky, and Yiza and Arian slept. Then the lorry pulled up, the driver switched off the engine, and they woke up. They woke at the same time. They were hungry. They weren't frightened.

But they didn't crawl out from under the tarpaulin. They heard voices. They didn't understand the language of this country. The voices didn't sound angry. They didn't sound good, either. Then the cover was thrown back. Beautiful sunlight fell onto the truck bed. Yiza and Arian didn't see it. They were lying under their tarpaulin. Just once, Arian worked his finger through the folds and peered out. He could see it was very bright. But that was all. Yiza whispered in his ear, and he whispered in her ear. I can't understand you, he said, be quiet, don't say anything else. But she went on whispering. Until he put his hand over her mouth.

The lorry was being loaded with palettes. Men were pushing them to the back and piling them one on top of another. No one paid any attention to the tarpaulins at the back, by the cab wall. The palettes were pushed close together, eventually filling the whole lorry. The cover was strapped on and the lorry pulled away. Arian and Yiza didn't have much room to move now. The drive shaft beneath them made the floor warm.

A little light came in through the rips in the cover. And a stream of cold air. They pulled up their hoods, not worrying about what would happen next. They sat close together. Hemmed in by the palettes and the back wall of the lorry, they couldn't move much. They couldn't change places. But they didn't worry; for a little while everything was good. There were jars in the palettes. Filled with edible things. Peaches in juice. Pears in juice. Cherries in juice. In the palette underneath were tins of peas, tins of beans, tins of carrots and peas. Tins of pearl onions. Arian pulled a jar of peaches out from one of the palettes. He tried to unscrew the lid. He couldn't do it. Yiza couldn't do it, either. Arian pulled out a tin of peas. He opened it by pulling the metal ring. He pocketed the lid. He handed the can to Yiza, squeezed it so that the rim formed a little spout, and showed her how to drink the peas. He took a second tin, and they drank and chewed peas and looked each other in the eye all the while. The portions were small, they didn't sate their hunger, and they each ate a second and a third tin. They pocketed the lids and the empty tins.

They were feeling slightly sick. They would have liked to sit beside each other and stretch their legs out. But there wasn't room for that. And so they sat opposite each other, their legs pulled up. They breathed cautiously and didn't move. They were frightened of being sick. They leaned back and fell asleep. But they didn't sleep deeply. They could feel it when the lorry went round a bend or stopped at a traffic light or drove down pot-holed roads. The peas were salted, their thirst woke them.

Arian, Yiza whispered. She shook his leg.

Arian propped himself up on his elbows and used the palettes to pull himself upright. Yiza, he said.

Arian. Nothing, she said.

They pulled their legs in even further and leaned forward so their faces were close together.

With one hand, Arian unzipped Yiza's coat, touched her stomach gently with his forefinger. Good? he asked. Good? He undid his coat, touched his forefinger to his own stomach and said firmly, in a deep voice: Good! Good! Then hers again: Good? His own, firmly: Good! Hers, gently: Good?

Good, said Yiza in Arian's language. She rubbed her belly. Good. Once more, she said: Good. This time in her language. And Arian copied her in her language. It was another word they had in common. Nothing. Good.

Their thirst made them unhappy and anxious and fidgety. Arian knew how he could open the jar of peaches. If he'd had a nail, for instance, he would have hammered it into the lid, with a stone, if he'd had a stone. Then the lid would have been easy to twist off. But he didn't have a stone, or a nail. And he didn't have a knife, either. He would have liked a knife. He had seen some very beautiful knives. He dreamed of owning his own knife.

Knife, he said. His tongue was sticky. His lips were sticky. Knife, he said, articulating each letter.

But Yiza was too thirsty to want to learn a new word. And Arian was too thirsty to teach her a new word. And how was he supposed to explain what the word meant when there was no knife there for him to point at? He tried to twist the lid off the jar again. He couldn't do it. The peaches wouldn't quench their thirst, anyway. The thirst had arrived suddenly. They were warm. But it wasn't a good warmth. It had come with the thirst. He reached for Yiza's hands. She slapped him away. She thrust out her lower lip. She wanted to be even smaller than she was.

I want a drink, she said. She knew Arian didn't understand her.

There's nothing I can do about that, he told her. It was easy to guess what she had said.

Then the lorry stopped. They heard voices again. This time there was laughter as well. The cover was thrown back. Light shone in, all the way to the back. The children wriggled back under the tarpaulin. The palettes were dragged across the floor of the lorry, and a forklift truck picked them up and took them away and came back for the next ones. Arian grabbed what he could, two jars, two tins. Eventually the tarpaulins by the back wall were all that was left. No one had any interest in them.

Arian rolled up one of the tarpaulins. It was almost two metres long and unwieldy – he wouldn't be able to carry it alone. He dragged it across the back of the lorry. Yiza followed him. She was whimpering again. Arian couldn't bear it. But there was no time to explain that to her without putting his hand over her mouth, and he didn't want to do that. He peeked through the cover and jumped off the lorry. He lifted Yiza down. He tucked one end of the tarpaulin under her arm, and held onto the other. They walked across the yard like that.

They didn't know where they were. They saw people standing by a wide gate and smoking. The people looked over at them. That was dangerous. They saw other lorries, and the forklift moving back and forth between them. The people all glanced over, but they seemed to have no interest in them. Arian thought that was because of the tarpaulin. It looked good, the way they were walking across the yard with the tarpaulin. It looked like they had a job to do. And so Arian slowed down. He had the jars and tins in his pockets. They were weighing his jacket down. Yiza wasn't whining any more.

On one side of the yard was a building, and looking along its concrete wall they could see lots of parked cars. The building was topped with huge words in lights. Now Arian knew they were behind a supermarket. He knew there was a lot of food there. And toilets with taps you could drink from. And he might find a nail. He could find a stone anywhere.

Good? he asked.

Yiza didn't answer.

After they had drunk, Yiza was happy. Arian had never seen such a happy face in his life. He could have seen his own face in the toilet mirror. It didn't interest him.

The tarpaulin was yellow. It was made of woven material coated in plastic. There were black letters on it. Arian couldn't read them. But he knew what letters were. Along the side of the tarpaulin were eyelets as big as coins. The tarpaulin protected them. With it, they looked like an adult had given them an errand to run. They carried the tarpaulin and people thought, these children have been asked to carry a tarpaulin, we mustn't stop them. Arian could see it in the faces that turned towards them.

They carried the tarpaulin through the supermarket, up and down the escalators. They strolled along the grocery aisles with it. Once, Arian stopped and looked at Yiza. She was solemn and weary. He shook his head. He put his face close to hers. And smiled. His eyes didn't smile, but his mouth did.

Do this, he said. This!

Do this, she said in her language.

This, he said and pointed to his smile. Do this!

Do this, she said. But she didn't smile.

He lifted the corners of her mouth with his thumb and forefinger.

This, he said, do this!

Then Yiza smiled. Her mouth smiled and her eyes smiled. Do this, she said in Arian's language. Do this.

Do this, he said.

Then they carried on down the grocery aisles, doing this and carrying their tarpaulin.

The rolled-up tarpaulin could hold a lot of things. First Arian slid in the tins and jars that had been making his coat so heavy. The tarpaulin sagged in the middle, but that didn't matter. When he and Yiza moved closer together, it was straight again.

The children marched as if they were going somewhere. Now and then Arian put something into the tarpaulin. An apple. Another apple. A banana. Another banana. Some bread rolls wrapped in plastic which were meant to be baked at home. A plastic bottle of water. Because he wanted to see Yiza's happy face again when she drank. They marched past the checkout and left the supermarket and walked across the carpark in the cold sunlight, as if someone was waiting for them and their tarpaulin. Someone important. Someone who had some clout. Who had sent them to bring him this tarpaulin. And nobody was allowed to stop them.

Perhaps this man who had sent them lived in one of the villas lining the hill that led up from the other side of the street. Perhaps he had a garage they could stay in. Some garages had radiators. Or a shed. Or a basement. Basements sometimes had radiators, too. Or heating pipes you could lean against.

They were looking forward to the food so much that the tarpaulin felt only half as heavy as it was. Arian held it so that Yiza was carrying the lighter part. The road with the villas on it was steep and paved. Snow was still lying in the shade. There was a danger they might slip over. Then the good things would fall out of the tarpaulin and roll into the street, and maybe someone would be watching from a window and call the police. The sun shone on the back of Arian's neck, he felt its warmth, he couldn't see a cloud in the sky. He looked forward to the food and imagined what it would be like, and couldn't remember all the things he had put in the tarpaulin, and he felt like he was about to get a surprise, as if they were hurrying to be somewhere and people were waiting there to give them presents.

As the road became steeper Yiza walked in front and Arian pushed her from behind, and she let him push her. She asked him something – he didn't understand, but he thought she was asking if they were nearly there, and he replied: It won't be long now, Yiza, we'll be there soon. I can see the house already, Yiza – and Yiza didn't understand him, but she thought he knew the way, and thought he'd said they would be there soon. Her name was the only thing she had understood, Arian had said it twice.

The villas lay behind low walls topped by cast iron railings. The villas' gates were tall and forbidding, like hinged walls, without handles. They didn't meet a soul. There were very few cars parked on the steep road. The trees were leafless. The last villa was on the edge of a wood. Its garden sloped steeply upwards, and had sets of steps and little walls running across it. The rose bushes were wrapped in jute sacks. It was the grandest villa on the hill. This was the end of the road.

Where the garden finished and the woodland began, there was an old greenhouse. They could see it from the end of the road. Its panes glinted in the sunlight. The side walls were made of bricks, with ivy growing up over them. The front and the roof were glass.

Arian couldn't see what was inside the little house, the panes were clouded.

That's good, he said. He was talking to himself, but Yiza nodded. He pushed her forward.

The tarpaulin was getting heavy. They walked on, side by side, and climbed up the slope at the end of the road. Their feet slipped on the slick, black, frozen weeds. Yiza held one side of the tarpaulin with both hands, and Arian held the other with both hands. The belly of the tarpaulin, where the good things were, dragged behind them. They dragged it into the woods.

The garden was separated from the woodland by a wire fence. It was two metres high, and topped with barbed wire. The ground beneath the fence was soft and uneven. In one place you could wriggle under it. If you were small. And if you were thin. They were. And if you shovelled the leaves and soil aside with your hands. They did.

The children unrolled their tarpaulin and threw the food over the fence. Yiza managed to get things over, too. She threw the tins and looked to see where they fell. She was the first to crawl under the fence. Arian rolled up the tarpaulin and pushed it after her, and Yiza pulled it through. Then Arian followed. They packed up their things again and dragged the tarpaulin behind the greenhouse, where it was shady and damp and cold. They couldn't be seen there. From the street, or from the villa.

They waited.

Yiza was waiting for Arian to do something. Arian didn't know what he was waiting for. He felt sick with hunger and exertion. He would have liked to eat a piece of the good bread that they had packed back into the tarpaulin. Or the apple. His apple. Or his banana. But he wanted them to be comfortable when they ate. As if they were at home.

He signalled to Yiza that she should wait and not move. Then he edged forward along the side wall. From the villa there was a clear view of the greenhouse. If anyone saw them, they would call the police. The police would come without making a sound, they'd grab Yiza first, then him. But they had no choice. It was going to be a cold night. In winter, when the sun shone in the daytime the night was icy. They had to get into the greenhouse. They would freeze to death outside. Arian hoped the door wasn't locked. He darted out from behind the wall, pressed the latch down, disappeared inside, closed the door. He caught his breath. Waited for his heart to stop hammering so hard against his ribs. Didn't dare look around. Then he crept back to Yiza. She was crouching there just as he had left her, sitting on her heels, her hands inside her coat sleeves. The tarpaulin in front of her. She coughed. The sun had just reached the greenhouse, like a spotlight shining on it. Arian pushed one end of the tarpaulin into Yiza's hands and held onto the other.

In a minute, he said. Let's wait one more minute.

Rich people live here, she said.

When I say: Now!

Rich people have horses, said Yiza.

Don't cough, he said.

We have to make sure we don't get sick, Arian whispered.

Once I saw a horse that didn't belong to anyone, Yiza whispered back. It was light and dark, light and dark.

Shamhan said we should get hold of some aspirin. Just in case.

It had a mother and a father, but no people.

Those are tablets.

No people.

Tablets.

No people.

One day you're going to understand what I'm saying, Yiza. I won't have to teach you. That's how it works. Suddenly you'll be able to talk like me. And I'll talk like you.

It was standing in a field. I was in the car and I saw it. It didn't move.

Don't talk any more now, Yiza.

I was looking out of the window.

I don't understand you.

Arian.

Stop talking now, Yiza.

Then I couldn't see it any more.

Now!

They crept along the side wall past the ivy, dragging the tarpaulin, hunched over as if that would make them invisible. They disappeared through the door like two shadows. As if a pair of buzzards had flown over the garden, casting their shadows.

Old frosted glass, the panes held in with lead. Some had been smashed and replaced. The new ones were plain. Arian pointed his finger at them. He showed Yiza what she mustn't do: move so that she could be seen from the villa through the clear glass. If she did that, she would die. He jerked his thumb across his throat. That meant die. She understood. But then they sat together by one of the clear panes after all, and watched the sun go down. They ate peas from the can and their apples and bananas and their rolls. And drank water and lemonade. Yiza coughed again. Arian pressed her face into the sleeve of his jacket.

Shh!

They closed their eyes to stop themselves being blinded by the sun. They listened to the crackling sound around them. Yiza put her hand into one of the flowerpots. She did it cautiously so Arian wouldn't hear, because she thought she was doing something naughty. The pot was full of dry soil. The soil was warm. A withered stalk stuck out from the middle of the pot. A leaf, light as wasp-paper, hung from a strand of cobweb. It was turning in the heat rising from the soil. Yiza dug her fingers into the soil and felt the cold where the sun hadn't reached. She quickly pulled her hand out of the flowerpot and hid it in her coat.

Arian's eyes were still closed. He could feel the warmth of the sun on his face, feel his skin tightening. He thought of nothing.

The sun's globe touched the horizon. It spread out. Turned white. Trembled in the mist. The children watched. Now their eyes could bear it.

The greenhouse was no longer in use. Forgotten things had withered there. The concrete floor was cracked, stained, yellow and rusty. One side of the little house – and that was lucky, that was really lucky – was fitted with a sturdy, raised wooden deck. There were earthenware pots on it, stacked one inside another, along with the watering can, work tools, shovels, hoes, spades, rakes, a paper sack full of gravel, half a bag of garden peat.

Help me, said Arian.

He showed Yiza what to do: she had to take the empty flowerpots to the other side of the greenhouse. She could carry two medium-sized pots at once. He took the other things. She kept coughing. They worked in silence, without a glance at each other. Soon it was too dark to find space on the other side. They spread the tarpaulin out on the wooden deck. They wrapped it around themselves twice. Soon they were asleep.

Yiza coughed. She sat up and coughed, and it sounded as if she was about to be sick. She stayed upright and slept sitting up. The coughing fit hadn't woken her. She had pulled the cover off Arian, and the cold woke him. He pulled Yiza back down. She was stiff and shivering a little. The moon shone on her face. Her eyes were shut, and she was asleep.

Put that there, he said softly to himself. Like that, yes, that there. And then that over there. And that. Like that, now. One there, one there.

He lifted the coughing Yiza and laid her on his chest. He turned his neck so that her mouth was in the hollow of his collarbone. Because the air is warmest there. It's the cold air that makes someone cough. And lying on a cold surface. Are you asleep? She didn't reply. And what could she have said, since she didn't speak his language? He clamped her hands under his armpits. Her hands were cold, but her head was hot.

The moon turned everything white. The window panes, which were already white. The flowerpots on the other side of the greenhouse. Arian was frightened of them. Particularly the big pot he had dragged over there himself. Three wispy hairs grew out of its head.

He wished Shamhan was there. He wished he could talk and have someone answer him. And he longed for his five Euro note.

He dreamed that the five Euro note called out for coins, and coins came, and it called out for notes, and notes came.

They woke when it was still dark. Arian wriggled his head out from under the tarpaulin. Belly and chest and face and the air between him and Yiza were warm. His back and legs and the nape of his neck were cold. When he took a breath, he could feel its iciness all the way down into his lungs. Yiza's head was burning. She had a fever. Her hands were still cold. She was shivering. Her teeth chattered. Arian had to uncover her in order to get out from under the tarpaulin. She pulled her knees right up to her chin. A little light shimmered through the white panes. He put his face close to hers. She looked at him. But there was no expectation in her eyes.

He took the thimble off her thumb and pulled off the plaster. He thought the cut looked better. He took her hand and put the thumb in her mouth. He placed the thimble in her other hand. She closed her fingers round it and shoved her fist into her pocket.

He explained what was going to happen. He pointed to himself, knocked his knuckles against his chest. I, he said. Knocked on her chest. You, he said. I, he said. I. Then he pretended his index and middle fingers were legs, marching across her chest, from one collarbone to the other. I, he said, I go. You see, that's me going. I go. I go soon. He moved his index and middle fingers away from Yiza's chest and onto the tarpaulin. I go away. Then the fingers came back, leaping from the tarpaulin onto her chest and marching from one collarbone to the other again. I come back. I go away. And come back. Away and back. You, he said, you. He folded his hands and placed them against his cheek and closed his eyes and smiled and rested his head on them, as if he were blissfully happy, and moved his head close to hers and made snoring noises. You. You sleep. I go, you sleep, I come back. He showed her that he wanted to go and fetch things to eat and drink. Put his thumb in his mouth and made drinking noises, pretended to eat with bulging cheeks. And that he wanted to fetch aspirin. That was difficult and not obvious, and he didn't know if she had understood him.

Aspirin, said Yiza. Her eyelids drooped.

Arian screwed the cap off the water bottle, put one hand behind Yiza's back and helped her sit up. She drank, water trickling from the corners of her mouth. He opened a tin of mandarins, fished out one piece after another and put them in her mouth. He drank the juice himself. The rolls were hard now, and sandy.

He pressed one into her hand, but she didn't want to take a bite. So he bit a piece off, chewed it, spat the warm, soft dough into his hand, and she licked it up. He wrapped her in the tarpaulin, dragged the large flowerpots over and stood them in front of her. Only the biggest ones.

He crept out of the greenhouse. Closed the latch. Crawled under the fence and ran down the dark path.

There was a metro station not far from the supermarket. He got on the last carriage and ducked down between the seats at the back. But then he thought: that's not good. If you duck, it means someone's looking for you, and he sat on the seat, but he didn't feel comfortable there. And ducked back down. And then sat back on the seat.

For the first few stations he was the only one on the train. The closer they came to the city centre, the more people got on. He could see it wasn't yet six o'clock in the morning. He wanted to be a good father-figure for their little household.

He didn't know which city he was in. He remembered which station he had got off at. He remembered which direction he had come from. He was quite good at remembering the shapes of words. He took a long look at the area around the metro station. There was a bridge in front of him. He couldn't see the river. A bakery to the right; the scent wafted over to him. An illuminated red sign above the door. When the sun came up, the sign probably wouldn't glow any more – he had to factor that in, experience told him things looked different when they weren't lit up. In the middle of the pavement was a newspaper stand, an octagonal building with a roof like the top of a church tower. That was the safest landmark.

Just then, the newspaper seller stepped out. He saw Arian, reached into his pocket and gave him a coin.

Aspirin, said Arian.

What?

Aspirin.

Aspirin?

Aspirin.

Are you sick?

Aspirin.

The man turned round and disappeared into his kiosk. He didn't come out again. You couldn't just stand around outside. It was too cold.

The coin was enough for a currant bun. At first, Arian only meant to eat half of it. But as he was chewing he forgot about that and three bites later the bun was gone. He would have liked to stay in the bakery. He had hoped lots of people would be standing in front of him, waiting, so he could warm up. But he had been the first and only customer.

Two women came towards him. Warm hats on their heads, scarves round their throats, boots, and short, thick jackets. He held out his hand.

Aspirin, he said.

What did he say?

Aspirin, he said.

He wants aspirin. I think he said aspirin. Do you have an aspirin?

Why does he want aspirin?

Aspirin, said Arian. But he didn't say it again. He walked on. His hand was so cold he couldn't hold it out in the open air any more, he didn't want to. He hid his hands in the sleeves of his jacket, and inside the sleeves he pulled his hands underneath his jumper and his shirt and warmed his right hand under his left armpit and the left under the right. And he walked on. Turned down an alley, away from the river. He thought the cold was coming up from the river.

One of the women ran after him and gave him two coins. For aspirin, she said. That should be enough. Her fingers touched his. She turned round and ran back. As if she was afraid of him.

If he hadn't been alone, he would have cried. Alone, he never cried. By this evening I want to have: aspirin, two currant buns, preferably four. Candles. Good food. Like sausages. Meat in a tin. Two tins. Bread. Butter. Bananas. He ran through the process of how he would heat up the meat in a tin over the candles. He would plant the candles in a flowerpot, so their light wouldn't be seen down at the villa. At least three candles. As many as possible. Then he would open the tin. Then he would wind two pieces of wire around the tin, so that the four ends of the wires stuck out from the tin in all directions. He would rest the wires on the rim of the flowerpot, and the tin would be suspended over the flames. He had seen some wire in the greenhouse. So he didn't need to get hold of wire. He would bend another piece to make a cooking spoon, and two more to make forks. He was excited. He was excited about going back to Yiza. He knew she would praise him. Warm meat and aspirin would make her better. He went through the process over and over again. Perhaps he could get milk and yoghurt, too. And cheese. And chocolate.

It was too cold. He ran back down the steps into the metro station. But it was too cold there as well. He got on a train. It was one of the new ones. He could walk from the last carriage to the first without having to get off in between. On the one hand that was good, Shamhan had told him, because you could see a ticket inspector coming a long way off. But on the other it wasn't so good, because you couldn't play cat-and-mouse with the ticket inspector. But Shamhan had preferred the new trains. Plus, the new trains had better heating.

Arian pulled his hat down over his forehead so the passengers couldn't see his eyebrows. Then he went from one to another, looking each one in the eye. Holding out his hand to them.

Aspirin, please.

After he had been down the train twice, he had collected twelve Euros and seventy cents. He also had four tablets. He could hardly believe it. He waited two stops, sitting right at the back, watching passengers leave and passengers get on. Then he conducted his experiment. He pulled the hat back down over his eyebrows, went from one passenger to the next, looking each of them in the eye.

Please, he said. This time all he said was: Please.

He went down the train again twice. He got one Euro and thirty cents.

He went a third time, this time without his hat on, so they could see his eyebrows.

Twenty cents.

He had discovered a trick all by himself. The greatest people were the ones who had invented a trick. They were the greatest. He was one of the greatest. He thought he understood people. They were afraid of his eyebrows. And someone begging for aspirin was new to them. That was the trick: bringing people something new. He had brought something new to the streets. He would have liked to tell Shamhan about it. In the afternoon he went to the river. He couldn't remember exactly where he and Shamhan had met for the first time. He thought he could remember, but then everything looked the same. He marched up and down for an hour, a hundred metres one way, a hundred metres back again. In one direction the sun was in his face, in the other it was on his back. But he didn't meet Shamhan. Maybe this wasn't even the same city.

He had thirty-four Euros and ten cents. He climbed into a lorry and stole two blankets, white and soft as a cat's fur. Lorry drivers seldom lock their doors, Shamhan had taught him, but car drivers always do. He wrapped everything he could get for his money in the blankets, and a few more things besides. A pharmacist had given him a big box of aspirin for free. After he had used the trick on him as well. Even the pharmacist had fallen for the trick.

There was a tap in the greenhouse. Yiza had tried to turn it on. She couldn't do it. She was thirsty. Arian was stronger than she was, and he managed it. The water was rusty. He put a bucket under it so the floor wouldn't get wet. That would definitely not have been good. After a while clear water came out, icy, clear water. Yiza had sweated through all her clothes. She was still feverish. Arian stripped her naked, wrapped her in the soft white blankets and folded the tarpaulin over her. Just as he had planned, he stuck half a dozen candles into a flowerpot, rinsed out an empty can, wound the wire round it and heated up some milk. Yiza drank cautiously. He showed her that she might cut her lip on the rim of the can if she wasn't careful. She was careful. He filled the can with water, made the water hot, wiped off the soot and gave her the can to warm her hands on.

The sun went down, but they had light. The candlelight coming from the flowerpot. That was their light. The flowerpot sat between them, and the candle flames warmed them.

Arian heated up some cat food in the can. He ripped the labels off first. He needn't have. Yiza liked the cat food, and she would have liked it even if she had known it was cat food. There was bread, too. In a little supermarket he had shoved a twelve-pack of the cat food, wrapped in plastic, under his shirt. It was only later that he'd seen the cute kittens on the labels. He had thought it was human food. They had bananas, too. And aspirin. It had been a good day.

In the night Yiza curled up in a ball, and Arian lay behind her and warmed her back with his belly. He held her little feet in his hands and rubbed them. He kept rubbing them even in his sleep. Sometimes he had to lift the tarpaulin to let in fresh air. Yiza coughed, and it sounded hollow and manly and strange, as if there were someone sitting inside her chest. Arian reached for the can of water and pulled it under the tarpaulin. The water was icy cold, even though he'd boiled it over the candles before falling asleep. He lifted Yiza's head and gave her a drink from it. Cold, she said in her language. But Arian understood her and remembered the word. He wrapped Yiza in both blankets and crawled out from under the tarpaulin. He was so cold his teeth chattered and his arms and legs trembled. The candles in the flowerpot had burned down to stubs. He lit them with the lighter, filled the can with fresh water and hung it over the flames. He crawled under the tarpaulin and cuddled up to Yiza, who was now like a ball of wool and didn't stir. When the water was hot, he hung a teabag in the can, and Yiza took it in her hands and drank in little sips.

Tea, she said in her language.

Tea, he said in his.

Tea, she said. Arian tea. She smiled and coughed.

Aspirin, he said.

She nodded, and he gave her a tablet.

Yiza?

Yes.

Are we dreaming?

I think we're dreaming, Arian.

Are we dreaming the same dream?

We're dreaming the same dream, Arian.

And you can understand my language?

You understand my language, too, Arian. We're grown-ups, Arian.

Maybe you're my wife.

I'd like you as my husband, Arian. You look after me. You protect me.

In the evenings we would listen to music. Have you ever listened to music, Yiza?

No, not yet. But I will listen to music. And I'll cook for you, Arian.

Have you ever cooked, Yiza? Rice or pasta, little balls of meat?

No. But I'll learn how. Do you like football, Arian?

Yes, I like it a lot. It must be wonderful to score a goal. Scoring a goal in an important match, that must be wonderful.

Yes?

Yes.

What can *I* do, Arian?

What do you mean, Yiza?

So that people praise me like they praise a footballer who scores a goal in an important match.

I don't know, Yiza. People don't praise women.

Would you praise me?

If you were my wife?

Would you praise me if I was your wife, Arian?

I would, Yiza.

Every day?

I would praise you every day, Yiza.

I'd praise you every day, too, Arian.

Sleep now, Yiza.

We *are* sleeping, Arian.

Sleep now.

They had enough food for the next day and enough candles, too. Arian had gone into a café and taken the teabags as he walked past the counter, putting them in his trouser pocket. And had then forgotten about them. He remembered them in the night. He hadn't thought about sugar. But he had thought about chocolate. He thought Yiza refused the chocolate because she knew he loved it so much. But then he saw that she was just giving a slight shake of her head. That she wasn't thinking anything. That she was feeling even worse than she had in the night. He took off his socks, kneaded them in some cold water and laid them on her forehead. She drank tea and ate bananas and apples. And swallowed aspirin. She coughed hard, and when she had finished coughing there were tears in her eyes, and she smacked her lips and swallowed and spat. He lay down beside her, pulled the tarpaulin over their heads and told her things in his language, unimportant things that no one would have wanted to hear if they understood his language. But Yiza didn't understand his language, and she liked to listen to him. When he tired more quickly than she did, she tugged at his collar, and he went on talking. In the end he stopped saying words and just made sounds, emphasising them as if they were words and as if the words were stories. Then they both fell asleep at the same time. When Yiza woke up because she was thirsty, he helped her sit up and put the can of tea to her lips. He had a bite of chocolate. And a drink of cold milk. And chewed bread for Yiza, who licked it off his hand.

On the third day Arian begged well and stole well and was given sausage and bread for free and a big bag of sweet pastries that were too stale to sell. When he walked back into the greenhouse in the late afternoon, before sunset, there was a woman there with Yiza in her arms. And the woman shooed him away. He dropped his haul and ran. Ran off down the road without looking back.

The woman carried Yiza down the garden to the villa. She descended the stone steps carefully, she put one foot in front of the other on the gravel of the winding paths, she kept pausing and balancing out her load so she didn't stumble, she was a petite woman, not very strong and not young any more, either. She said: My little one, everything will be alright now.

Yiza stood in the bathroom, naked, wrapped in a towel. The woman put a hand under the water coming out of the bath taps to check the temperature.

In a minute you're going to feel like you're in heaven, she said. The bathroom was spacious; the bathtub was freestanding and rested on cast iron feet shaped like a lion's paws. The walls were tiled in a soft shade of vanilla. There was a mirror in three sections above the sink. The room smelled of perfumed soap.

I'm going to wash you and put some cream on you, said the woman. Then I'm going to get you into a clean bed, and you're going to sleep and get better.

Yiza didn't look at her. She didn't look at anything. She wasn't cold any more. She wasn't hungry. She wasn't thirsty, either. She was tired. She wasn't thinking about dreams and she wasn't thinking about Arian.

Her feet seemed a long way off. As if she had grown in the last few hours.

Come on, said the woman. Come on!

She took off the towel, led her over to the bathtub and made a sign. Yiza got into the bath. Sat down in the water and stared straight ahead, just as she had before. The woman stopped talking to her for a while, she just gestured. Then she felt it was too quiet, and started talking again.

That's your head, said the woman, soaping Yiza's head. Your head is made up of your face and your hair. But you know all that, don't you?

She put a finger under Yiza's chin and tilted her face towards her. But Yiza looked through her.

My poor child, said the woman, it's a good thing you came to me. My name is Renate. I'm Renate. Renate. Renate. I'm Renate, who are you? My name's Renate, what's yours? And those are your shoulders. And that's your neck. That's your chest, that's your back. And that's your hand. These are your fingers. What have you got in your hand? Show me! Open your hand! Can I see, please? Open your hand.

Yiza opened her hand and showed the woman the thimble.

Beautiful, said the woman. I'm not going to take it away from you. We'll put it here. When we've finished our bath, you can have it back. There it is.

Yiza didn't let the thimble out of her sight while the

woman washed her, and when she got out of the bath, she picked it up again at once.

The woman dried Yiza, rubbed moisturiser into her thin body, wrapped the towel round her and carried her into the bedroom. She put a nightshirt on her and tucked her in. She sat down in an armchair in the corner.

You don't understand me. Or do you? If you understand me, could you nod your head? Or put a leg out from under the covers?

But Yiza didn't nod, or put a leg out from under the covers. She coughed, and it didn't sound good. Soon she fell asleep, and soon it was a new day.

The woman gave her tea to drink and porridge or lightly salted potato soup and steamed carrots. She tucked a thermometer under her arm. When her temperature rose to 40 degrees, she laid cloths soaked in vinegar on her calves. It's a good thing you came to me, she kept saying, and then it was evening and night and morning again and evening again and night again.

Yiza was dreaming, or else she wasn't: A man was standing in the doorway, looking at her. His arms hung down by his sides. His head was tilted slightly to one side. He was far away, but also close by. His head reached past the top of the doorframe. He was wearing dark clothes. She fell asleep looking at him. She would have liked to say her friend's name, but her lips wouldn't make any sounds. She had hidden the thimble under the mattress. Pushed it in as far as she could reach, so it was underneath her head.

The man was standing in the doorway again. The door was wide open this time, and there was a light on in the hall. This time the man was shorter, his head didn't touch the doorframe. Yiza heard voices. The voices came from behind the man. But the man didn't say anything. He looked at her with his head slightly tilted to one side.

On the fourth or fifth day her fever broke. She drank a lot. Sat up in bed, propped on the huge scatter cushions. She held the cup with both hands. She drank hastily, and red tea dripped onto her clean nightshirt. She glanced hurriedly up at the woman sitting beside the bed, to see if she had noticed her carelessness. The woman smiled and nodded and closed her eyes.

Yiza woke in the night. The woman wasn't in the room any more. There was a chamber pot beside the bed. A small lamp gave out a dim light. She hopped down onto the floor and walked up and down, up and down. The room had two doors. Both were locked. There were some biscuits on the bedside table, next to the lamp – two coated in chocolate, two in melted sugar. She didn't touch them. But she drank all the water in the carafe.

She climbed onto the windowsill and opened a

window. Icy air streamed in. Her chest was wet with sweat and the cold stung her skin. She couldn't climb down into the garden, it was too far down, and everything below was black. She quickly shut the window again. She would have liked to take the biscuits out to the greenhouse so that Arian could eat them – he would have enjoyed them. The window looked out over the valley. She thought she could see the lights where the supermarket was, but she wasn't sure.

She looked under the bed. It was too dark to make anything out. She listened. She pulled the covers off the bed and lay down on the floor. She couldn't sleep, and sat on the chamber pot. Her hand smelled of the cream the woman had rubbed into her. The woman had scrubbed her fingers with a brush. She had cut her nails and dipped her hands in scouring powder and scrubbed them again, this time with an even stiffer brush. But her fingers hadn't come clean. The nails had been cut down to the quick.

She fell asleep on the chamber pot and toppled sideways, and the contents spilled over the wooden floor. She crawled into a corner of the room and wrapped herself in the bedcovers and fell asleep.

She slept.

And woke as the man picked her up and carried her to the bed. He stood there for a while before lying her down on the fresh, white sheet. She was happy that the man was holding her. He smelled like her uncle.

Yiza had breakfast in bed. That was what the woman wanted. She wanted to watch her eat. She wanted to look at the pale little face and the black hair, which was short now and gleamed like satin. And she wanted to look at the starched white shirt, the sleeves and the little collar with the embroidered edges and the mother-of-pearl buttons down the chest. She placed a little bed-table on the covers in front of her, on top of it a tray with a cup of tea and a bread roll cut in half and spread with butter. She had realised now that her darling didn't like sweet things. She scattered the crumbs onto the windowsill outside.

Come here, she said, look, she said, and showed her the sparrows. One of them looked at Yiza with his tiny all-black eyes.

When Yiza was well enough that she didn't have to spend all day in bed, the woman took her by the hand and led her out into the hall and along the hall to another room.

The woman said: Five! Five minutes! This will only take five minutes! She counted on her fingers. One, two, three, four, five! Five!

She led her to a chair, pressed her into it, stroked her hair and smiled, making the lines show on her face.

This room was filled with furniture. Yiza had never seen furniture like this. It smelled of hot spices in there. The windows were hung with curtains, they were dark and heavy. The woman leant over Yiza and wouldn't let go of her hands. Yiza tugged, but the woman wouldn't let go of her hands. Yiza whimpered, but the woman wouldn't let go. Yiza dug her fingernails into the woman's thumb. The woman cried out, let go of Yiza's hand, put her thumb in her mouth and slapped her in the face with her other hand.

Yiza put her hands over her eyes. She started to breathe faster and faster. The woman leant over her and said she hadn't meant to do that, unlike Yiza, who had quite deliberately bitten her hand. There were footsteps in the hall. Things bumped against other things, a door was opened and closed again.

Don't breathe so fast. Stop that!

But Yiza went on breathing so fast.

I'll have to hit you again to make you stop, said the woman. Or you're going to faint on me.

Yiza was taken back to her room. A table and two chairs were now standing in the middle of the floor. On the table were an exercise book, some colouring pencils and a box with brightly-coloured writing on it. There were new clothes hanging over one of the chairs, for her to put on. White underwear. White tights. A red jumper. A red skirt with white polka dots. Red slippers with white dots as well.

No one has worn those before you, said the woman. If only I knew your name. What's your name? Me: Renate. You? You? You?

The woman repeated the You, and with every You she tapped Yiza's chest with her forefinger. A little harder each time.

Yiza said: Arian.

Your name's Arian? You Arian? The woman tapped Yiza's chest again. You Arian?

Yiza shook her head.

But the woman was content. The child had spoken at last. She had said something at last.

Tomorrow you can put on your new clothes, she said. Today you sleep. Then we'll eat together. Then you sleep. Then you put your new clothes on. Then we'll do lessons. Then you'll learn my language. Then we'll live together. You'll see.

The curtains stayed closed during the day as well. They left only a small strip of light. She could see blue and branches. Yiza watched day become night in a darkened room, as the strip of light was extinguished. Until outside and inside were the same. Until everything was the same. A weak, golden glow from the bedside table where the lamp stood was the only thing that was different. It was easy to dream with your eyes open there. When she lay in bed, sleeping and waking were the same. Everything was the same. In her dream Arian spoke like her. And she spoke like Arian. There was no difference. In the dream she talked a lot and waved her arms like her uncle had done when he talked a lot. She walked beside Arian – once he was Shamhan, then he was Arian – it was all the same, and she was the same as everyone else, too. There were noises in the night, outside her door, in the hall, voices, and once she thought she heard the man laughing.

Call me Granny, said the woman. That's easier than Renate. Granny. Say Granny.

Yiza said: Granny.

The woman made a tick in an exercise book. Like in a game of cards, when you've won. The first word.

Say hand.

Hand.

The second tick. That had been easy.

Say tongue. Where is your tongue. Open your mouth. Look: my tongue. That's my tongue. You have a tongue, too. Where is your tongue? Say tongue. Show me your tongue. Tongue.

Tongue.

Show me your tongue. That's your tongue, yes, there it is.

Tongue.

The third tick.

Who am I?

Granny.

What's that?

Hand.

Where's your tongue?

Tongue.

You're tired now.

Tired.

What is tired?

Tired.

But you need to know what tired is, not just the word, you have to think. This is tired. Look here. Don't look over there. Look at me. This is tired. Look here. This is tired.

Tired.

You can say it. But do you know what it means? What does tired mean? Do tired!

Tired.

Now you're tired. Yes, now you're tired.

It was still winter then.

In spring, at the end of May, Yiza looked out of the kitchen window one evening and saw Arian standing down below on the street. It was still light enough for her to recognise him. He was looking up at the window. He recognised her too. He quickly stepped into the shade of the hedge.

She pretended to yawn, and moved her head like the woman did when her neck ached with tiredness. She did that to seem like she was just looking around aimlessly, and not looking out of the window. She said she needed the toilet, could she go please, and then flinched because she had asked, and she wasn't supposed to ask, the woman got angry when she asked if she could go to the toilet, that made it sound like Yiza was afraid of her, like she didn't allow Yiza to go to the toilet, she was supposed to just get up and go to the door and wait by the door until the woman got up and went to the door as well, and then wait until the door was unlocked.

Yiza's heart was pounding so loud she was afraid the woman would hear it.

The woman got up slowly from the kitchen table, she was always full of aches and pains. She reached into her apron pocket and got out the key, held it in her hand, held it out in front of her as if she was already aiming for the lock. Yiza snatched the key from her hand and gave her a shove that made her grab the sink to stay upright. Yiza unlocked the door, pulled the key out of the lock, darted out into the hall and locked the kitchen from the outside.

The woman hammered on the door and shouted at her, and Yiza was frightened of the voice and clenched her fingers together.

But then she ran down the stairs and out of the house, she was in her socks, she ran across the paving slabs outside the house, called out to Arian and opened the gate to the street.

She spoke to him in the woman's language. And Arian answered in the same language.

Yiza took him into the house. She held his hand. He was fearful and let her pull him along and didn't want to go, but she dragged him. She dragged him upstairs to where the kitchen was.

The woman on the other side of the door said: Open up, Yiza! I promise you.

Yiza didn't understand what she was promising. And Arian didn't understand it either.

Arian pressed a finger to his lips. He whispered in Yiza's ear.

Show me! Food, he whispered. Hungry. Show me! Please, show me!

Yiza whispered back and showed him. She pointed a finger, which was very clean, at the kitchen door. She whispered that the food was in the kitchen and the woman was in the kitchen and the woman was very cross.

Arian whispered that she should talk to the woman. Talk. Say. And so on. He demonstrated what he meant. He moved his forefinger in a circle like a wheel and opened and closed his mouth. That was supposed to mean: and so on and so on and so on, don't stop. It was supposed to mean: in the meantime he would... He turned round and went into one of the rooms, came straight out again, went into the next room, left the door open. But Yiza didn't talk to the woman.

The woman said – and her voice was quite calm now – Yiza. I know you're by the door. You abused my trust. Now we'll both have to start all over again. Another few days and we wouldn't have needed the key, no more keys, imagine that. That was going to be the surprise I told you about. And a few days after that we would have gone out into the garden together and done some planting. And in summer, you would have been allowed into the garden on your own. Now we have to start all over again. But I expect this is the end of everything now. Yes, I think this is the end. Do what you like, Yiza, it's over now. I'm going to open the window and shout for the police. Is that what you want, Yiza?

Then Yiza screamed and didn't stop.

Arian ran past her. He was carrying something.

He turned the key she had left in the kitchen door, and Yiza fell silent.

The woman put her head out and her blue collar. She was bending down so that her face would be on a level with Yiza's when she saw the child. She stared into the darkness and smiled when she saw Yiza's face. She opened her mouth as if to say something nice, showing the teeth that Yiza knew so well, and the big soft lips that she knew so well. Arian swung his arm back and struck the thing he was holding against the woman's forehead. He hit her again straight away. He was screaming like Yiza had screamed. He screamed the very same way, as if he was copying her. The woman stumbled into the hallway, threw her arms out, tripped and fell. Arian hit her a third time, this time on the back of her head. The woman twitched as she lay on the floor, she turned over, she was lying on her back now, her legs twitched, and her lips struggled to make a strange noise that did not become a word. Arian hit her a fourth time and a fifth time and a sixth time.

Yiza was sitting downstairs on the front doorstep. To her left and right were plastic bags full of good things, and a jumper, a pillow and a blanket. She was waiting for Arian. He had found a suitcase, and was filling that, too, with good things from the house. He definitely wanted to pack some candles and matches and a knife or two and a tin opener and a spoon, and definitely sugar. It was night-time now. And it was quiet. There was no one on the street. Arian knew what they were going to do. Yiza knew that.

They took the metro into the city. People noticed them because they had so much baggage. But no one asked questions; they couldn't see what was in the bags and the suitcase with wheels. Arian had pulled his hat right down over his forehead. Yiza didn't look at him. She wanted to keep her eyes closed, but she couldn't, they kept opening again. Arian had told her she should just sit there and not think about anything, and then no one else would think anything, either. It was difficult to say what he wanted to say in the foreign language. He had wanted to say he knew from experience that people looked you in the face if you were thinking about something. It wasn't *what* you were thinking, it was the fact that you were thinking. He had explained to Yiza how not to think. You just had to think of a single word. You had to say that word silently to yourself. Without moving your lips. Any word. For example, he thought *paper.* He didn't know exactly what the word meant.

But that was even better. He thought *paper*, always *paper,* since the winter he had been thinking *paper*, and it looked like he wasn't thinking. Could she think *paper* too, Yiza had asked, without looking at him. Would he mind. He wouldn't mind, said Arian. He smiled at her, but Yiza didn't smile back.

They sat on the train and thought *paper*. People looked at them, but they didn't ask any questions.

They got off at one of the stations down by the canal. Arian wheeled the suitcase, Yiza carried the bags to the escalator, and they waited there until they were alone. It was already late at night. Arian stuffed a piece of cake into his mouth and swallowed drily and was hardly able to breathe. He tried to catch Yiza's eye, smiling in advance so that she wouldn't miss his smile if she looked at him. But Yiza still didn't look at him. She looked away, and when he walked around her to stand in her eye line, she turned her head aside.

Give me an apple, he said. He didn't say *apple*, he said another word – he said a lot of words, until she finally understood what he meant.

She said: Apple.

He repeated: Apple. And smiled.

Arian knew what to do. In the bushes by the canal, there was a supermarket trolley. It was lying on its side, covered with the tarpaulin. The bank by the path was steep, you couldn't see the trolley from the path. At least, not at night. Did she remember the tarpaulin, Arian asked. Yiza nodded and then she looked into his dirty face for the first time. And looked away again at once. She took a corner of the tarpaulin between her thumb and forefinger.

Arian said: Yiza. He said: Yiza! He asked: Are you scared of me?

She nodded.

He said: I did that once before. No one messes with me. Not me! But you don't need to be scared, he said, and he asked again: Are you scared of me, Yiza?

Yiza looked away and said nothing and didn't nod and didn't shake her head. He told her again that no one messed with him.

It was hard work getting the trolley up onto the path. Arian instructed Yiza in his language, which she didn't understand. He told her not to just stand there and watch. Help me, he said in the language that was now their common language, though they only knew a few words of it, and he knew some words that she didn't, and she knew many more that he didn't.

First they pulled the tarpaulin off the shopping trolley and dragged it up onto the path. There were street lights all the way along the towpath. They made sure they were alone. Then they pushed and pulled the trolley up the bank and set it on its wheels. They heaved the suitcase into it, and the bags, and covered them with the tarpaulin.

If she was tired, said Arian, she should get into the trolley too, there was enough room for her, it was best if she lay down under the tarpaulin, he would push her, it was easy. It took a long time for him to put all this together in their shared language.

Yiza didn't want to. She walked behind Arian. But Arian didn't want her to. He told her to walk beside him, not behind him, he had to be able to see her. He didn't want anyone behind him. Then she got into the trolley and pulled the tarpaulin over her head. Without saying a word.

She reached into one of the plastic bags and found an apple and stuck the hand with the apple in it out from under the tarpaulin and waited until the apple was taken from her. She thought maybe he would take the thimble as well. But Arian didn't do that.

She called to Arian. He didn't hear her. But she didn't call loudly. She whispered his name. She was so tired that she struggled to get past the R. The trolley smelled of the bread from the pantry. Yiza had showed Arian where the woman kept the good things. She had hoped the woman would start screaming. At the same time she was afraid of it. The woman lay in the doorway like a long, low, grey hill. Arian said: That one and that one and that too, and that. She repeated his words now, under the tarpaulin, softly.

And then she was asleep, and then she was rising to the surface and sleeping again and surfacing again, like taking long, slow, happy breaths.

She thought she could see herself forgetting the

woman who had saved her life – that was how she'd referred to herself, as the woman who had saved Yiza's life. Yiza watched herself forgetting the room and the table in the middle of the room and the exercise book on it and fell asleep, raised herself up a little and fell asleep.

The shopping trolley's small wheels rattled beneath her, like a chain drive of loneliness, but without the lonely people who could have given order to the noises and named and categorised the cold or the heat. Aromas would form themselves into cravings; little fingernails would alleviate the annoying little pains. The little fingernails are still pink and white and neatly cut and filed smooth.

If it is true that God's favourite stands at his right hand, in everything he does, at everything he plants and blesses, if that is true, then hear the footsteps, the little ones, the big ones, the scampering and the stamping! Wait until your eyes grow accustomed to the dark! And now? Can you see them? Can you see the two of them?

The cool, warm night breeze blows through the bars of the shopping trolley.

A May night.

Arian is the captain. He is steering the ship towards his